"You really don't think Mr. Kingsley is good enough," Cecily concluded. "He wouldn't be good enough if he were seven feet tall."

"No one is good enough for our daughter. Not really." Father's smile was bittersweet.

Cecily sent a grateful smile to her father. At least he understood her.

"I have your best interests at heart too," Mother said.

"I know you do, Mother." Cecily told no lie. Mother had made a good match for herself. Wouldn't any reasonable mother want to see a repeat of such a successful history?

"Whether you admit it to yourself or not," Mother continued, "you have become accustomed to a certain lifestyle, one that requires that your future husband be well situated. Not only does Delmar come from wealth, but his schooling will assure that he will succeed on his own."

"I'm sure it will," Cecily agreed. "But what if Delmar isn't the one for me? What if the Lord wants me to learn the art of sacrifice?"

"As with many things the Lord wants from us, the art of sacrifice is more easily opined upon than practiced," Mother observed. "Lest you think your father and I are concerned merely about money, think again. What about this salesman's character? What do you really know about him, Cecily? We've only seen him a few times."

"I know that he's witty, and attractive, and charming. And most important, he loves the Lord."

**TAMELA HANCOCK MURRAY** shares her home in Virginia with her godly husband and their two beautiful daughters. The car is her second home as she chauffeurs her girls to their many activities related to church, school, sports, scouting, and music. She is thankful that several local Christian radio stations allow her family to spend much of their driving time in praise and worship. Tamela hopes that her stories of God-centered romance edify and entertain her sisters in Christ.

Books by Tamela Hancock Murray
**HEARTSONG PRESENTS**
HP213—Picture of Love
HP408—Destinations
HP453—The Elusive Mr. Perfect
HP501—Thrill of the Hunt
HP544—A Light Among Shadows

Tamela Hancock Murray

AUTHOR

Lovesweept

TITLE

| DATE DUE | BORROWER'S NAME |
|----------|-----------------|

**A note from the Author:**
*I love to hear from my readers! You may correspond with me by writing:*

> **Tamela Hancock Murray**
> **Author Relations**
> **PO Box 719**
> **Uhrichsville, OH 44683**

**ISBN 1-58660-934-3**

**LOVESWEPT**

Our mission is to publish and distribute inspirational products offering exceptional value and biblical encouragement to the masses.

All Scripture quotations are taken from the King James Version of the Bible.

All of the characters and events in this book are fictitious. Any resemblance to actual persons, living or dead, or to actual events is purely coincidental.

PRINTED IN THE U.S.A.

## one

"Please stop singing through your nose, Miss Eaton. Think of yourself as a nightingale, not a parrot."

"But, Professor Tobias," Cecily protested in defense of her sister's off-key performance, "parrots are ever so much more interesting."

Augusta slapped a hand over her mouth to suppress a giggle but removed it as soon as she composed herself. "All right, Professor Tobias. I'll try to do better."

Professor Tobias looked down his nose at Cecily. The sternness that had just darkened his long face dissipated. "Why don't you show Miss Augusta how to sing the scales properly, Miss Cecily?" He placed a long forefinger on middle C.

Before Cecily could comply, the doorbell chimed. Seeing a chance to escape the lesson, Cecily lifted her ankle-length skirt ever so slightly and flounced from the parlor before Professor Tobias could object.

"I'll get it, Hattie," she called to the maid from the foyer.

When she flung open the door, she was greeted by a burst of cool spring air and a salesman. His diminutive stature made her conscious of her six-foot-tall frame. Yet his face wore a rare mixture of kindness and confidence. Ebony eyes nearly made her swoon.

"Good morning, Miss!" He tipped his hat.

As their glances met, Cecily could discern his interest in her. Such attention was unusual. Most men, especially those who stood fewer than six feet in height, took one look and ran. The pride of the men she knew, spurred by the expectation that men should be taller than their mates, limited Cecily's choice of suitors. She didn't mind short men. They simply were the ones who wouldn't give her a chance.

Cecily's close friends and family assured her that she was beautiful. In her most honest moments, Cecily admitted to herself that her face was pleasant enough. She thought about her friends who were of the age to court. They looked pleasant too. Most of them were of a diminutive, and thus desirable, stature. Even so, Cecily found company and conversation at every event she attended. She supposed the Lord could have given her a heavier cross to bear than her height.

She glanced at the salesman once more before averting her eyes to the points of her shoes. She noticed that his eyes twinkled with a kindness and generosity of spirit she never saw in strangers. Could he possibly think her pretty?

"Averil Kingsley at your service." His voice didn't resonate with the southern drawl familiar to Virginia's capital city. The melody was much too chipper. Enchanted by its urgency, Cecily looked up in time to see him sweep his arm outward, allowing a sunbeam to sparkle off a gold cuff link. "And a fine morning it is. Wouldn't you agree?"

Cecily peered past Mr. Kingsley's shoulder. She had to agree. A slight breeze rippled through the air, carrying the faint scent of blooming flowers across the lawn. The tall pines that had marked her front yard ever since Cecily could remember swayed back and forth. She noticed that the sky appeared to be cerulean blue. Fluffy white clouds, reminding her of soft cotton, floated upon the canvas. She nodded twice. "Yes. Yes, I would. I would say it's a beautiful day indeed."

Cecily clasped her hands and nervously swished her thumbs together. It wasn't like her to repeat herself. To her ears, she sounded like a blathering idiot. What was she thinking?

The lilt of Augusta practicing scales drifted into the foyer. Averil's face relaxed as though he were enjoying the performance. "And a fine morning it is for music."

"That's my sister. I take lessons with Professor Tobias too," Cecily hastened to add.

He clutched the handle of the machine he carried. "I'm sorry to have interrupted. Should I return another time?"

She managed to stutter out a word that sounded like no.

"Are you quite certain?" His eyes were pleading.

"Yes. Yes indeed. Quite certain." There she went again, repeating herself.

"Wonderful. My business with you will be brief." He stepped back, revealing a machine. The salesman swept his arms above the contraption, presenting it as though it were an exotic grand prize. "This is the new, the fantastic, the only one of its kind manufactured today." He paused, apparently for effect. "I present to you—the Capital Duster Electric Pneumatic Carpet Renovator."

Cecily stared at the machine. She felt certain she'd seen a similar beast in one of Mother's periodicals. It looked heavy and cumbersome, though she did find its shade of deep blue appealing. Touching the verandah was a cylinder that looked as though it housed the carpet beater. An engine rested above, and a wooden handle protruded from the top. A long blue bag was attached to the engine.

"Isn't she a beauty?" He ran his hand over the bag as though he were petting a favorite feline.

Cecily didn't know how to answer. How could any household equipment be considered beautiful, even if it did come in a nice shade of deep blue? "I suppose you might call her a beauty." She placed her right forefinger on her cheek and studied it again, searching for an answer that wouldn't be a lie. "Yes, I suppose as household products go, she is a beauty."

"I'm pleased that you agree. And did you know that you will be among the first homes here on Monument Avenue to possess one if I take your order today?" He held up his hand. "Don't answer that. Being the envy of the block is not the best reason to purchase a pneumatic carpet renovator. But sanitation and hygiene are two very good reasons. Doesn't your family deserve the cleanest, most hygienic environment you can provide them?"

"Why, yes. I believe they do." Cecily nodded.

"Then you've come to the right place."

"But, Mr. Kingsley," Cecily couldn't resist pointing out, "you are the one who came to me."

He chuckled. "How right you are. I must say, you don't miss a trick." He lifted his forefinger. "And that is good for me. Very, very good. Because that means you are a smart woman who knows the value of an excellent household product."

"Go on," Cecily prodded, amused by his flattery.

He didn't hesitate to comply. "This pneumatic carpet renovator removes household dirt from carpeting, upholstery, tapestries, draperies, hardwood flooring, and sundry household items."

Cecily's heart felt as though it were falling to the bottoms of her high-top shoes. She wanted to buy a pneumatic carpet renovator. If it would please the comely and charming Averil Kingsley, she would buy one for each floor of the house, including the cellar. Maybe she would buy one for each room. But no. Mother would never agree to purchase a new carpet cleaner. Not even one.

Cecily swallowed. "I can see you have faith in your product, Mr. Kingsley. In fact, I don't think I've ever seen a salesman more sincere about what he was selling."

Averil beamed, obviously pleased by her words. "I seem sincere because I am. I'm no snake oil salesman. I represent a fine product, one that I use myself." He raised his forefinger. "May I add that my own mother uses the Capital Duster Electric Pneumatic Carpet Renovator. And she is very fond of hers. Very fond. That's why I have full confidence that each and every customer of Capital Duster Company will be pleased with this product."

"I'm sure Mother would be. But I'm afraid we already have a carpet cleaner, Mr. Kingsley." Cecily allowed herself a regretful sigh.

His expression didn't become defeated, as she had expected. Instead, he kept his demeanor coolly confident. "I'm sure you don't have one like this." He looked both ways and leaned closer, but not too closely. Just far enough so Cecily would get the impression that she was becoming privy to a huge secret. "This is no ordinary pneumatic carpet renovator. This one runs on electricity."

Cecily stepped back and clasped her hand to her lace-covered throat. "That is impressive!" Perhaps Mother would consider buying one, after all.

"Will you allow me to step in and demonstrate? I won't take but a few short minutes of your time."

"Certainly." Cecily stepped back to allow him to enter. The scent of bay rum followed him.

"Might I ask you to show me the machine you use to clean your carpets now?"

"Of course." Cecily led Averil to the room off the side of the parlor. Augusta's chirping indicated the voice lesson continued to progress. On the side of Father's overstuffed chair stood what appeared to be a wooden side table. In fact, the table opened up to reveal a hand-pumped carpet sweeper.

Averil folded his arms across his chest as he eyed the sweeper. "Perhaps this was an inheritance from your grandmother? A Whirlwind model from the War Between the States, perchance?"

"The War Between the States?" She didn't bother to conceal her surprise. Certainly Mr. Kingsley knew his carpet renovators better than that! She would set him straight. "No, Mr. Kingsley. It's only about ten years old."

"Only ten years, eh?" He shook his head. "How quickly man advances." Averil cast Cecily a consoling look. "Thankfully, you wisely purchased a model that doubles as a fine end table. That way, it will still be of use once you've replaced it with the Capital Duster Electric Pneumatic Carpet Renovator."

"I suppose. . ."

Averil didn't wait for Cecily to consider the possibilities. "Now then, could you run this old sweeper over your carpet? Just once will be enough for my demonstration."

"I'm not sure I know how. Hattie usually does that for us." Unwilling to be deterred, Cecily called for Hattie, who soon appeared.

"Hattie," asked Cecily, "will you run the carpet sweeper for Mr. Kingsley?"

The maid placed her hands on stout hips. "Now, Miss Cecily, you knows I don't do no sweepin' without your momma. It takes two of us to run that sweeper."

"I can help you, Hattie," Cecily offered.

"What for?" Hattie's eyes narrowed when she spotted Averil and his new carpet renovator. "He tryin' to sell you a new machine?"

"I just thought I'd see what it does and tell Mother about it when she gets home."

Hattie eyed Averil. "Mista, we don't need no new contraptions heah today. If you's a thinkin' you can sell one here, you'll jes have to come back another day."

"He just wants to show us," Cecily objected.

"Uh-uh." She shook her head vigorously, throwing both hands in the air. "I ain't havin' nothin' to do with this, Miss Cecily. You need to wait till your momma gets home." She pointed to the parlor. "An' you need to get back to your music lesson."

"I will, as soon as I see how the new machine works."

"Uh-uh! Uh-uh!" Shaking her head, Hattie exited the room, still voicing her objections as she returned to the kitchen.

"I thought you seemed quite young to be the lady of the house," Averil noted. "I suppose I should have asked first."

"No, that's quite all right. I probably should have told you earlier." Cecily felt a sudden blush of embarrassment warm her cheeks.

Averil let out a sigh of defeat. "I don't suppose it will do either of us any good for me to waste your time, then. I'll return later."

"I hate for you to have gone to all this trouble and not even give me a demonstration. Do let me see the carpet renovator anyway." She flashed him what she knew to be an appealing smile. "If it works as well as you seem to think it does, I'll be sure to tell Mother all about it."

"Are you sure you don't mind? I hate to be party to you missing your music lesson."

"I don't mind. We're concentrating on voice at the moment, and I much prefer to play the piano. And my sister certainly never minds if I have to leave the room during the lesson."

"Oh?"

Cecily grinned and whispered. "She's sweet on the instructor."

"So now I'm part of a conspiracy." He made his observation with an amused expression, a twinkle entering both eyes. For the first time, Cecily noticed that when he smiled, his cheeks dimpled in a most pleasing way.

"You may be able to say that."

"In that event, I'll set up your old cleaner. Let me do the pumping, and you can run the nozzle over a rug. Preferably one that sees a lot of traffic."

"How about the rug in the foyer? That sees more traffic than any other, I suppose."

Minutes later, the mission was accomplished.

Cecily wiped a forearm over her forehead. "I didn't realize how much work this is. Mother always makes everything look so easy."

"That's what mothers do. So don't you think she deserves to own the best pneumatic carpet renovator made today? Not to mention, the whole house will be more sanitary and hygienic."

"Really?"

"Do you have any reason to doubt?" He waved his hands back and forth. "Don't answer that. Let me set your mind at ease this minute." He lifted a forefinger in the air. "Now, here is where the ordinary salesman with an ordinary product will simply sweep behind you, showing you how much dirt your old machine leaves behind. But I'm so confident in the superiority of my product, that I will go one step further." He opened a small metal box he had been carrying that turned out to contain several attachments, some papers, and a bag. Averil reached for the bag. With flourish, he opened it and proceeded to dump a mound of dust and dirt all over the rug.

"Mr. Kingsley!"

"Now, now. Not to worry. This will all be gone in the wink of an eye. Just watch." He searched the walls, looking for an electrical wall sconce.

"Over there."

Grandly, he screwed the plug into the sconce. "You will be amazed by how quickly this dirt will disappear when I use the pneumatic carpet renovator. Your newly hygienic, sanitary, dirt-free home begins with a flick of a switch."

He moved the switch to the "on" position. No noise came from the machine. The beater bar didn't move. Nothing. Averil's dark eyebrows shot up while his mouth closed into a frustrated line. He moved the switch up and down several times. Still nothing.

Cecily looked at the mound of filth on her mother's prized Oriental rug, the same rug that had rested in her grandmother's foyer.

"I don't know what's happening." Averil's distress was evident as he kept moving the switch back and forth. He finally unplugged the machine. Then, turning it over, he inspected it. "I don't see anything clogging the beater bar or any other reason why this machine shouldn't operate." He looked up at Cecily. "It worked just fine at the last house. In fact, I even sold one to Mrs. MacGregor next door, using the very same demonstration I was about to give you."

"But I thought if I bought one, I'd be the first one on the block to own a Capital Duster."

A look of chagrin flashed over Averil's features before he quickly recovered. "I did say that, now didn't I?"

Cecily folded her arms and arched her eyebrow in a most challenging manner. "Yes, you did."

"I'm so sorry." He looked deeply into Cecily's eyes and lowered his voice. "I beg your pardon for saying so, but as soon as I saw you, I forgot all about Mrs. MacGregor."

Cecily had been taught better than to laugh at such a fresh remark, but a girlish giggle escaped her lips nevertheless. After clapping a hand over her mouth, which so often betrayed her, Cecily fluttered her lashes toward the floor for a moment before introducing a slight change of topic.

"How unfortunate that the carpet cleaner doesn't work. Mother and Mrs. MacGregor are big rivals. If she knew Mrs. MacGregor bought one, you would have sold another one on the spot."

"Is that so? Then let me add that not only would your dear mother trump the neighbor, but also she'd be getting a bargain. The Capital Duster sells for only seventy-five dollars."

Cecily's hand flew up to her chest. "Seventy-five dollars? Isn't that a lot of money?"

Averil stood up to his full height, which still only brought his head to the top of her neck. "In most circumstances, I would tell you that seventy-five dollars is only pennies a day. But I know I've hardly convinced you of the need to buy a machine that apparently doesn't work." He observed the dirt he had thrown on the rug. "Please accept my deepest apologies, Miss, Miss—"

"Eaton. Miss Cecily Eaton."

"The least I can do is to help you clean up the mess I made. Would you be so kind as to allow me?"

"That's all right," she assured him. "Hattie can clean it later."

His lips tightened into a line indicating obvious chagrin. "If I remember correctly, she warned us against my little demonstration." He looked at the dirty rug. "I'm afraid she was right." Mr. Kingsley returned his gaze to Cecily. "I made this mess. I'll clean it up."

Cecily nodded. "All right. If you insist."

As he disappeared into the study to retrieve the old sweeper,

Hattie entered the foyer, dust rag in hand. When she spotted the dirt, her eyes widened, and she let out a screech. "Miss Cecily! What happened?"

"Don't worry. Mr. Kingsley will clean it up."

"That man ain't gone yet? Don't he know when he's not welcome? Looks like he could take a hint." She shook her finger. "You tell him he better clean this up, and good. Your momma prizes this rug. She won't be too happy iffin that dirt don't come out."

Cecily knew Hattie was right. Yet she wasn't worried. Averil would get the dirt out with the old cleaner. And no one would ever know he had been here. Except her. She sighed. Averil would leave, and he would have no good reason to come back. That meant she would be stuck with tiresome old Delmar. So what if Delmar stood more than six feet tall? He was the only man she knew who stood taller than herself, but that was all that could recommend him. Hardly the basis for true love. Cecily grimaced.

The screen door flung open, interrupting her thoughts. Cecily's brother, Roger, hurried in from giving the dog a bath. "Got to get another bucket of water for Elmo," he explained.

"Don't step in that—"

Too late. Roger's bare foot, drenched in soapy water, had already sunk into the heap of dirt. Roger let out a yelp of disgust and placed his other wet foot on another part of the filthy area. Unable to recover, Roger stepped on several places on the rug, creating a path of brown footprints.

Not knowing what else to do, Cecily yelled, "Roger! You're ruining the rug! Get out! Get out! I'll bring you the water."

Nodding, Roger turned and headed out the doorway. As the door opened, Elmo took the opportunity to burst into the house. Oblivious to any mess, the dog bounded over the rug, carrying what had become mud along with him. The result was a path of paw prints beside the footprints that Roger had left.

Apparently curious as to the cause of the commotion, Augusta and Professor Tobias entered. "What's happening?"

Augusta's gaze fell to the rug. She let out a horrified gasp. "Mother's rug! It's ruined!"

"I—I'm sure we can get it straight."

Augusta shook her head, her eyes wide as her hands flew to her hips. "What do you mean, we? I had nothing to do with this. I was taking my music lesson." As though she suddenly remembered the instructor was standing beside her, Augusta turned her face upward and fluttered her long eyelashes at the bespectacled blond professor of music.

He seemed not to notice the interest of his young student. "Miss Cecily, I insist that you return to the parlor for the remainder of your lesson."

"I will, just not now. Not until we get the rug cleaned."

At that moment, Hattie entered the foyer. "I sent that dog out the kitchen—" As soon as she saw the rug, she slapped a hand to her cheek. "What happened here?"

"It's all right, Hattie. Mr. Kingsley will get it cleaned up."

"What's he waitin' for? The Lord's second comin'?" She shook her head and muttered, "Why, I have half a mind to—"

"Please, Hattie. Don't worry. He'll clean it up. I promise," said Cecily.

"I don't see how." She shook her head in wonder. "All right, but I'm tellin' your momma I had nothin' to do with this. Nothin'. And I mean nothin'!"

Cecily was relieved when Averil, who in her mind had taken on the role of Knight in Shining Armor, entered with Mother's hand-pump carpet sweeper. "Everyone, please leave," she commanded confidently. "Mr. Kingsley and I will clean the rug now."

They obeyed with varying degrees of reluctance. "All right, Mr. Kingsley," Cecily told him, "you pump, and I'll run the nozzle."

The salesman stood frozen in place.

"Would you rather I pump and you run the nozzle?" she ventured, wondering why he hesitated.

Averil had paled so that his eyes seemed darker than ever. "It doesn't matter. This dirt isn't coming up."

Cecily's heart felt as though it leapt into her throat. "What do you mean, the dirt isn't coming up?"

"The pneumatic carpet renovator is meant for dry dirt. Not anything wet." His brown-eyed gaze met hers. "I thought I heard a big hullabaloo out here. What happened?"

Cecily explained, hoping against hope that as she spoke, Averil would think of a way to rid the rug of dirt. Instead of the hoped-for solution, Averil just shook his head and kept staring at the mess. "I don't know what to do, Miss Eaton. I have no idea how to get this rug clean. Perhaps we could let it dry and try sweeping it up then."

"We don't have time. Mother is due back from her ladies' temperance meeting any minute. We've got to get it clean now."

"Yes, I certainly am due back from my meeting," Mother's voice intervened as the front door snapped to a close behind her. "What is this about getting something clean?"

Cecily turned to face her. "It's. . .it's the rug."

She watched her mother's gaze travel to the large, wet spot. Her mouth dropped open, and she gasped.

"Mother, I'm sorry—"

Though her mother didn't speak, rage was evident in her expression. "Cecily, what is the meaning of this?" Her hand swept toward Averil. "And who is this man?"

Cecily opened her mouth to answer. Before she could speak, her world turned to total darkness.

# two

Cecily awakened to the pungent odor of smelling salts. Augusta was kneeling by her side. Cecily could see the ceiling of the foyer. When she discovered her breathing was easier than normal, she realized her corset had been loosened.

"I thought I was the only one in this family allowed to swoon," Augusta whispered.

Cecily sent her sister a weak smile. Augusta was in the habit of tightening her corset beyond human endurance whenever Professor Tobias was due for a lesson. Often she would forget to loosen it to its normal size after the lesson, resulting in the occasional fainting spell. Cecily was about to ask her sister what had happened when the memory of the disastrous morning began to fill her mind. She recalled all too well.

"How are you feeling?" Augusta asked.

"A bit puny." All the same, Cecily tried to sit up. The sudden motion made her dizzy.

"Take it easy." Augusta placed a hand underneath Cecily's head. Cecily laid back into it, letting her sister ease her back into a supine position.

"Is she going to be all right?" the salesman asked.

"Mr. Kingsley?" Cecily looked in the direction of the pleasant baritone.

He knelt beside her. "I'm so sorry to have caused you such trouble. I assure you, the Capital Duster Company will make proper restitution."

"You are right about that." Mother's arms were folded across her ample chest. She gave the salesman a narrow-eyed stare. "No one comes into my house to demonstrate an inferior product, ruins my rug, and then leaves without making things right."

Regardless of how Mother felt about the salesman's promise, Cecily was charmed. How silly of her to feel that way over someone she didn't even know. What was the matter with her? "Of course he'll make it right, Mother," Cecily said in his defense. "I just know he will."

Mr. Kingsley looked down upon her, his face filled with gratitude. Such a sweet reward! Just his unspoken thanks were enough to make her think she might swoon once more. She managed a smile in return, but her happiness was short-lived.

"I don't know what you've said to my daughter to cause her to take leave of her senses," Mother said, "but I demand that you leave this instant."

"Poor Mr. Kingsley." Cecily sat upright. This time, she fought the lessened dizziness and remained vertical.

"There, there. I thank you for your concern," he said. "Not to worry. What might I do, Madame, to make proper restitution with you?"

"My husband handles all our business affairs."

"Very well. I shall be back this evening, then, to settle matters with him. Would that arrangement be favorable to you?" he asked.

"Certainly." Mother's voice was chilly.

Cecily's shoulders slumped. She didn't envy Averil a confrontation with her father.

"I bid you all a good day." Averil tipped his hat to the ladies.

"Good day, Mr. Kingsley," Cecily said cheerily. She tried to rise to her feet, but felt too dizzy to complete the task.

"Sit back for awhile yet," Augusta advised.

"Yes," Mother agreed. "You need time to recover."

"Let me try again."

"Are you certain?" Augusta asked. When Cecily nodded, her sister took her by the crook of the arm and guided her to her feet. "What do you care whether he comes back or not? He's just a door-to-door salesman." Her tone indicated her disapproval.

"But it's all my fault. I insisted that he demonstrate the pneumatic carpet renovator even though Mother wasn't here to buy one, and it led to such a terrible mess."

"None of that is your fault," Augusta answered. "After all, who would have thought the carpet cleaner wouldn't work? And the dog tracking mud all over didn't help matters."

"I know, but I must shoulder my part of the blame. Even if it means I have to do extra chores for a month." Cecily's voice betrayed her lack of enthusiasm. She wasn't eager to face her mother after she had contributed to the carpet's ruination.

"Augusta, bring her into the kitchen for some tea," Mother called.

"Tell her I don't want any tea," she whispered to Augusta.

"Don't be silly. You have to face her sometime. Might as well get it over with."

&

Averil sat on the edge of the bed in his shabby boardinghouse room. Ever since he had left the Eaton house, all he could think of was Cecily. He prayed she had recovered from her swoon. He and his renovator that didn't work had been to blame for her sudden spell, not to mention the ruination of an heirloom. Certainly Cecily was angry with him. How could he have been such a failure?

Sighing, Averil observed his lodgings. He wasn't accustomed to such meager surroundings, but the little room was all he could afford on his savings. His father had insisted on paying him on commission, just as he paid the other door-to-door salesmen who labored to sell the carpet cleaners he manufactured.

"I want you to know what it's like to start at the bottom, Son," he had said before forcing Averil to launch his career in the family business. "You'll begin by working with the cleaning staff for six months. Next, you'll go selling our product door-to-door, just as all the other salesmen do."

Averil Kingsley Sr. promised his son he was doing him a favor by giving him the Richmond, Virginia, sales territory to start. Averil wasn't so sure. New York City was a larger area with more wealthy households. However, his father was adamant that he start a new campaign in the southern states. Since Richmond was the first city of the South, they couldn't think of a better place to begin marketing in the region.

"When Father finds out what happened today, he'll put me to work in the factory, emptying rubbish," Averil lamented. "How can I tell him the Capital Duster failed at the second house I visited?"

As always when he was discouraged, Averil reached for his well-worn Bible. One of his favorite passages was in the twenty-fourth chapter of Luke, the incident where Jesus visited His disciples after His resurrection:

"And as they thus spake, Jesus Himself stood in the midst of them, and saith unto them, Peace be unto you. But they were terrified and affrighted, and supposed that they had seen a spirit. And He said unto them, Why are ye troubled? and why do thoughts arise in your hearts? Behold My hands and My feet, that it is I myself: handle Me, and see; for a spirit hath not flesh and bones, as ye see Me have. And when He had thus spoken, He shewed them His hands and His feet."

As Averil continued reading, a feeling of peace enveloped him. No matter how upset Father might be, and even if Averil showed himself to be the worst salesman in the world, it didn't matter. As long as he walked with the Lord, God's plan for his life would unfold.

At that moment, Averil felt led to get down on his knees and appeal to God for help. "Lord, maybe Thy plan is not the same as my earthly father's plan. Maybe Thou didst not want me to be a salesman. If that is so, Thou didst not waste time showing me." Averil paused. "Lord, please guide me and strengthen me, no matter how much I seem to fail. In the holy name of Thy Son, Jesus Christ. Amen."

Averil rose to his feet and consulted his pocket watch. Six o'clock was nearing. If he left now, he would have just enough time to reach the Eaton house and settle his business with Mr. Eaton before he would have to return to the boardinghouse for dinner. He had already sent a wire to Father, but not enough time had passed to receive a response. Nevertheless, Averil knew he shouldn't delay in settling matters with the Eatons. He needed to pay for the replacement of their rug. He only hoped the cost wouldn't deplete all of his savings before the commission from the MacGregor sale arrived.

After wiping suddenly sweaty palms on his handkerchief, Averil exited his sparse room and shut the creaky door behind him. He bounded down the narrow stairs, determined not to waste a moment getting to the Eaton house.

He had opened the front door to leave when he heard Miss Hallowell calling from the bowels of the kitchen, "Who's that?"

"It's just me, Mr. Kingsley," he shouted back.

"Will you be joinin' us for dinner, Mr. Kingsley?" Miss Hallowell called.

Averil cringed. The landlady's voice sounded like a cackle in comparison to Cecily's. "That's my intention, Miss Hallowell," he answered.

"I warn you, I won't hold dinner should you be late," she shouted.

"I shall be mindful of that fact."

Stepping off the stoop, Averil remembered Cecily again. His thoughts hadn't ventured far from her beautiful face since he had been forced to depart from her house. He imagined himself looking at her first thing in the morning across the breakfast table for the rest of his life. Light brown hair might still be unconfined from its chignon, falling to her shoulders. Or perhaps

Cecily was the type of person who relished the daybreak, rising early to prepare herself for the morning. Either way, he knew she would appear beautiful.

He imagined that Cecily's kind features would mirror her sweet voice, inquiring about the news in the day's paper. Though she would ask to show an interest in the things that were of importance to him, Cecily herself would be more enamored with the fashion and society pages.

He envisioned that once he had exited the house for another day of work and Cecily had begun her day of household duties, she would treat everyone she came into contact with—from the grocer to the lowliest maid—with as much respect and compassion as she had treated him that day. Averil had the distinct impression that Cecily regarded everyone from the least to the most important with the same attitude of genuine caring and concern. In her presence, he felt as though she could see him as more than a temporary nuisance, a pest to be rid of as soon as possible so she could get on with the important matters of her existence. He felt that she looked at him as a person worthy of dignity even though, as far as she knew, he was an ordinary salesman, unworthy of her notice.

Barely noticing the outdoors or passing buggies himself, Averil dreamed of Cecily as he walked toward her home. Not only was she the epitome of a sweet disposition, but also Cecily looked the picture of health and beauty. His imagination returned to the image of her loveliness. Her lustrous, light brown mane was set in a perfect chignon, leaving a cloud of hair to frame her heart-shaped face. Delicate brows set off to perfection her light brown eyes flecked with gold. A pointed nose interrupted smooth skin and pink lips that reminded him of the roses his mother grew in her garden.

Cecily was tall and regal. Too tall, in fact. How could he expect such a lovely, statuesque woman to look twice at someone of his diminutive stature? He had fantasized that she was looking at him with interest, her eyes lingering on his face longer than necessary. Perhaps that's all his musings were—fantasy.

He let out a resigned sigh. No matter. She perceived him to be a traveling salesman—no catch for someone in her social position. But no one could keep him from dreaming. At this moment, his idle thoughts were all that kept one foot moving in front of the other as he went to face the unknown Mr. Eaton.

Passing Mrs. MacGregor's house, Averil noticed that she was watering hanging plants on her verandah. "Good evening, Mrs. MacGregor." He smiled pleasantly and tipped his hat.

To his surprise, she stopped her task. "Wait just a moment, Mr. Kingsley."

Obeying, he froze on the sidewalk. What could she possibly want? Perhaps she had a question about her recent purchase. A feeling of confidence settled through him. Averil Kingsley Jr. was prepared to answer any question about the Capital Duster.

"Mr. Kingsley," she said as she approached, "I have something to say to you."

"Yes, Madame?"

"I want my deposit back."

Averil tried not to let his anguish show, but his faltering voice betrayed him. "You. . .you what?"

"I want my deposit back." She placed her hands on her hips and jutted out her chin. "I heard what happened at the Eaton house after you visited me."

"Oh." His gaze fell to the ground. "I was afraid of that."

"I suppose you were. Richmond may be a big city, but around here, we look out for one another, Mr. Kingsley. When a stranger descends upon us and sells defective products, word gets around. And now, I want my money back."

"But, Mrs. MacGregor, you have not even taken delivery on your carpet renovator. I'll be glad to give you your deposit back after thirty days if you're not satisfied. It even says so in your contract."

"As far as I'm concerned, that contract is not worth the paper it's written on. I no longer have any desire to try your product for thirty days, or even one day, for that matter. I simply want my deposit back." She extended her hand as though she expected him to produce the funds on the spot.

"I would really like to be able to accommodate you, Mrs. MacGregor, but the truth of the matter is, I cannot. I have already wired your deposit to my company. The money is no longer in my possession."

"No longer in your possession?" The older woman huffed. Standing at her full height, she looked down her nose at Averil. "Then I want you to contact your company first thing tomorrow morning and demand they send the money back! The entire seven dollars and fifty cents!"

"Yes, Ma'am. I'll be in touch." He tipped his hat.

"You'd better be!" With a toss of her head, the scornful customer turned her back to him and proceeded to take long strides toward her house.

The encounter had left Averil shaken. Losing a sale in such dramatic fashion would have been a disappointment at any time, but the loss was especially troubling in his current circumstance. With the cancelled MacGregor sale, Averil was left with no forthcoming commission. Combined with a carpet renovator that didn't work, he had no way of making any new sales. Plus he had to pay for a rug. The collateral damage was enough to make Averil want to return home, hat in hand, and admit to his father that he was a failure. A complete, abject failure.

With these despairing thoughts, Averil ascended the five steps to the Eaton porch. The windows were open, allowing him to hear a halting rendition of some classical piece being played on the piano. He guessed, based on his limited knowledge of music, that Mozart had composed the work. Whoever had written it, Averil surmised he wouldn't be honored to hear the piece played in such a stilted fashion. Missed notes and all floated into the air, disturbing what was otherwise a silent evening. Averil wondered if Cecily was playing. She'd told him earlier she preferred the piano to voice lessons. Somehow, he had imagined Cecily's playing would be flawless. . . .

"Evenin', Mr. Kingsley," Hattie greeted him as she answered the door. "Mr. Eaton's expectin' you. I'll go get him."

Averil tipped his hat. "Thank you." If he harbored hope that Hattie might invite him in, that idea was dashed as she turned around and sauntered down the front hall without so much as opening the screen door.

"Who was that, Hattie?"

Averil's heart began beating rapidly. That was Cecily's voice! Maybe she would invite him in for a cup of tea. He consulted his pocket watch. Supper time at the boardinghouse was nearing. The unexpected delay he had been forced to endure as a result of his impromptu visit with Mrs. MacGregor left him precious little time to conduct his business at the Eatons' before he would be obliged to rush home. He sent up a silent prayer that the confrontation would be brief and the settlement agreeable to all concerned.

"Never you mind, Chile," he heard Hattie call out.

Her answer left him with little hope he would even be able to steal a look at Cecily's face, much less linger over refreshment. The next instant, he heard footfalls that sounded like a woman's high-top boots clacking across hardwood floors. Only a moment flashed by until his dream appeared at the door.

"Well, of all things! Letting you stand out here like this. I'll have to speak to Hattie about that. Please accept my apology, Mr. Kingsley." Cecily motioned for him to step back, then opened the door.

He tipped his hat. "That won't be necessary, Miss Eaton. I'm sure your maid is aware this isn't exactly a social call. If anything, I should be extending my deepest apologies to you—and to her—for the uproar I caused here today."

"You were hardly alone in its cause, Mr. Kingsley. Father realizes that."

"So you've already explained things to him. How kind of you to intercede on my behalf. Truly, I am no villain."

She laughed, a dainty sound not unlike the melody of a harp. "There are no villains in this story, Mr. Kingsley. It's not as though you could be an evil banker calling the mortgage on our house, since there is none." She studied the room as though she were seeing it for the first time. "Grandpa Eaton built this place with his own hands long ago." Pride filled her voice.

Averil had been so occupied with selling the carpet renovator earlier that he hadn't taken time to notice the workmanship of the Eaton home. Wainscoting and crown molding decorated the edges of the foyer. Unlike the view in his boardinghouse room, not a crack was to be seen in the plastered walls. The hardwood floors were as even and polished as he remembered. A quick glance into the other rooms visible from his vantage point proved that the superior workmanship extended to the rest of the house.

"Your grandfather was talented indeed. This is a fine house." His words were sincere, and he could see that Cecily knew it.

"Thank you." She studied the foyer. "I cherish this place. Not that one should treasure things, mind you. You know what the Bible says about that."

Was she a believer, a true follower of Christ? Her Bible knowledge seemed to indicate so! In his excitement, Averil's words rushed forward. "Yes, I'm aware that our Lord and Savior said not to put our trust in things of the world—"

Cecily completed the quotation: " 'Where moth and rust doth corrupt, and where thieves break through and steal: But lay up for yourselves treasures in heaven, where neither moth nor rust doth corrupt, and where thieves do not break through nor steal.' "

"Yes," Averil said. "Exactly."

" 'For where your treasure is, there will your heart be also.' " Cecily looked thoughtful as she recited this part of Jesus' admonition.

"If your mother is as understanding about her rug as you are, I shall be a fortunate man."

"I'm afraid she's quite upset. I told her it's only a thing, an object," Cecily assured him. "But it was Grandmama's, and so she's in quite a mood over it. She shall recover."

The sound of heavier footsteps clomping toward the foyer interrupted their conversation. Averil was suddenly aware that his throat was dry. He swallowed. He was not looking forward to meeting the owner of the house.

# three

As Mr. Eaton approached, Averil saw that he was a tall man, which was no surprise considering Cecily's height. Cecily's father was large enough to be intimidating except for the compassionate expression in his light brown eyes with gold flecks that were a replica of his daughter's. When Mr. Eaton was close enough, he extended his hand.

"You must be Averil Kingsley."

"Yes, I am." Averil nodded and took the older man's hand. Mr. Eaton's grasp was firm and businesslike, not the least bit threatening.

"I understand you had quite an adventure here today."

Averil nodded. "And I do apologize, Sir. I hope you will allow me to make amends. I want to make everything right."

A ringing dinner bell interrupted their conversation.

"I see this is not an especially good time for you," Averil said. "I can stop by tomorrow."

He heard soft footfalls entering from the hallway. "Of course you may stop by tomorrow." Cecily sent an appealing look toward her father. In spite of his silence, or perhaps because of it, Cecily turned to Averil and gave him a devastating smile. "If you haven't had dinner, won't you stay here and dine with us? Our cook makes fabulous roast. That's what we're having tonight."

Averil suppressed a gasp. This vision of loveliness had broken convention by inviting him to dinner. Should he accept? The prospect of sharing a meal with Cecily was more than tempting. And now that the roast had been called to his attention, Averil noticed the delectable aroma of cooked meat wafting through the foyer. The food at his boardinghouse was better than average as accommodations of that sort went—at least, that's what the other boarders told him. Judging from the smell of the Eatons' anticipated meal, Averil knew for a fact that anything Miss Hallowell's cook conjured up wouldn't be nearly as delicious.

All the same, good manners prompted Averil to push aside his yearning to be with Cecily—and his sudden recognition of how hungry he was. "I appreciate such a generous offer, but I really shouldn't impose."

"Please do impose," Cecily insisted. "Unless you have a previous engagement." Her lower lip protruded into an ever-so-slight pout.

Averil was pleased to note the strain of disappointment in her voice and face. "I did promise my landlady I would be home for dinner."

His confession was rewarded by a disappointed look on Cecily's face. "Oh."

Her barely uttered admission spurred him into acceptance. "I must say, my landlady warned me she wouldn't hold dinner for me should I tarry." He extracted his gold watch from its accustomed place in his vest pocket and noted the time. "It seems I'm already running a few minutes late. I doubt my fellow boarders would miss me much should I not make my appearance. More likely, they'll be grateful they can divide my portion of the meal among themselves."

"Then I insist that you join us," Mr. Eaton said. "I can see that in both breeding and manners, you are far and above most of the salesmen we encounter. Surely you were reared to enjoy much better than boardinghouse accommodations."

"I must admit, this is my first boardinghouse experience," he muttered. Averil wasn't ready to share his life story with the Eatons. At least, not yet.

"I suspected as much," Mr. Eaton said. "I shall look forward to learning more about you at my dinner table. As I'm sure we all will."

Unwilling to seem too eager, he hesitated. "If you insist, then I shall be pleased."

"Good," said Cecily. "I'll tell Hattie to set an extra place at the table."

The dinner proved as delicious as Cecily had promised. Averil would have welcomed almost any chance to skip a meal at the boardinghouse, but in the company of such a vision as Cecily, the event seemed more like a fantasy turned into a pleasant reality.

Cecily leaned closer to him. Averil breathed the delightful gardenia scent she wore. "I hope this meal is at least as good as what you normally would eat."

He nodded with enthusiasm. "Far superior to anything I could hope to find at Miss Hallowell's."

"Miss Hallowell's? Is that where you are staying?" Mrs. Eaton interrupted.

What a time for her to decide to join the conversation! Averil wiped his mouth before answering. "Yes, Madame."

Her eyebrows rose. "And the accommodations are satisfactory to a man such as yourself?"

Averil wasn't sure whether Mrs. Eaton meant that he was too fine to be living in a boardinghouse or if the boardinghouse were too fine for him. Regardless as to Mrs. Eaton's opinion, his current accommodations were hardly his dream. Yet Miss Hallowell's was the best he could afford at the moment. "Naturally the house is nothing like home, but I make do."

"Perhaps you'd find the Swann more to your liking," Mrs. Eaton suggested.

Thankfully, Cecily's brother, Roger, chose that moment to distract Mrs. Eaton from Averil's exchange with Cecily with a question about whether he could play a game of catch before starting his math homework.

All the same, Averil inwardly cringed. Friends familiar with the area had recommended the Swann to him, but when he inquired, he found the accommodations too costly for his current situation. Although her mother's attention had been diverted,

Cecily looked at him as though she expected some sort of comment. "Perhaps the next time I'm in the city," he remarked.

"So you won't be here long?" Cecily asked.

She had asked a sensible question. He wondered why he had said something so misleading. Did he hear the faintest bit of disappointment in her voice? Did she wish he would be staying in the city indefinitely, or was his imagination working overtime?

He cleared his throat. "This is my sales territory, so I'll be here quite awhile, actually. I will have to leave the city upon occasion to visit other prospective clients, but as you can imagine, my primary clientele is among people in your social set."

Cecily furrowed her brow as she buttered a roll.

Why had he offered such a garbled explanation? "And," he added for good measure, "Miss Hallowell's is the closest boardinghouse within walking distance of here."

"Are you really obliged to walk everywhere, carrying that big machine with you?"

"Sometimes I make use of the streetcar," he said.

"I suppose that helps," Cecily admitted.

"Yes, but even though the Capital Duster Electric Pneumatic Carpet Renovator is as light as a feather, it can be a bit bulky to maneuver in such close quarters. I find it easier to walk most places, at least on the job." He lifted a forefinger. "However, I have been promised a carriage. I'm expecting it to be available in a week or so."

"A carriage! How impressive!" Cecily exclaimed.

"I hope so. It will bear a company sign. In blue letters, much like the color of the carpet renovators we sell." Averil concentrated on cutting his beef. "I hate to admit it, but I don't feel I've earned such a fine carriage. Salesmen aren't generally assigned a carriage until after they've sold at least ten units."

"But you are suffering difficulties, being asked to leave your home," Cecily pointed out.

"Dining here with you can hardly be considered a hardship." Averil grinned, then popped a small portion of beef into his mouth.

Cecily tittered in a delightful manner. "I'm certain you'll sell ten units, or even more, in no time at all."

"One can hope," he said. "The record for sales is held by Otto Foreman. He sold seven in one day. That was the old Model 128. He retired ten years ago."

Cecily's eyebrows rose. "You certainly seem to know a lot about the company. No wonder they have so much confidence in you."

Averil nodded, but he felt as though he were bearing false witness. If Father had true confidence in his capabilities, he would have taken Averil under his wing and trained him at corporate headquarters rather than choosing his opportunistic brother-in-law. Now here he was, banished to territory new and untried to Capital Duster. Here, he would have to make his mark.

"So," Cecily asked after taking a sip of tea, "have you been in the city long?"

"No. Yesterday was my first day in Richmond."

"In that case, I hope you enjoy getting acquainted with our city. I've lived here all my life, so I confess to a bit of partiality when I boast about its merits." Cecily glanced out of the window. "Such as the lovely weather we have here in the spring."

"Lovely indeed."

She set her cup in her saucer and pushed her chair away from the table. "Mother, it's so gorgeous outdoors today. I'm wondering if perhaps I can take dessert on the verandah."

"I'm sure that would be fine."

Cecily set her gaze upon Averil. "Perhaps you would care to join me, Mr. Kingsley?"

"Why, I most certainly would," Averil agreed.

From the corner of his eye, he saw Roger open his mouth. Without missing a beat, his father placed a warning hand on his forearm. Averil wasn't sure exactly why Cecily wanted relative privacy, but he had no intention of arguing.

"Hattie can bring out the tray," her father said.

"That would be fine, Father."

"Perhaps you would like some company," Mrs. Eaton suggested. Her eyes narrowed, their stare boring into Averil as though he were some evil being.

Mr. Eaton chuckled. "My dear, they don't need us old folks bothering them."

Averil watched Cecily shoot her father what appeared to be a look of thanks. He couldn't remember a time when any woman had showed such an interest in him without knowing he was heir to a significant business concern. The feeling was liberating. He relished it.

A few moments later, Averil and Cecily were sitting across from each other in matching white wicker chairs, enjoying apple pie and tea. The scent of a purple lilac bush in full bloom hung heavily in the air. Averil was grateful that the verandah roof sheltered them both from the afternoon sun. His friends in upstate New York might still be wearing shawls and light coats this time of year. In contrast, the Virginia sun could get strong at times, even though summer had not yet sighed its first breath of life. He envisioned that as summer waxed and waned, his fondness for tall glasses of minted iced tea would grow accordingly.

"So," Cecily asked, breaking the silence, "I'm sure this afternoon is one that you wish had not happened?"

"I share in your wish, but I believe in the product I sell, and I trust in the Lord to lead me to those who can benefit from what I believe to be the best carpet renovator manufactured today."

"That's good to hear."

"Which one?" he couldn't resist asking. "That I believe in my product or that I trust in the Lord?"

"Both. But especially that you love the Lord."

He nodded. The knowledge of her fine spiritual state warmed his soul.

Cecily leaned over toward him, not too closely as to be improper, but closely enough that he could smell her delightful gardenia scent. "So do I. And speaking of giving Him each day, I'm wondering. . ." She paused and took a sip of tea. Her brown eyes looked at him over the rim of the dainty china cup.

"Yes?"

"Since you haven't been here long, I'm assuming you have no plans as of yet for the Celebration of Spring?"

"Celebration of Spring?" Wondering where this was leading, Averil decided to hide his curiosity by taking a gulp of tea.

"Yes. Of course, there are many spring festivities all around the city, but why don't you come along with us to the celebration at the boys' school? My brother Roger is a student there. They—that is, a group of us ladies, not the boys—will be performing a Maypole dance, and the food is always quite good."

He looked up. "Sounds delightful."

She fluttered her lashes. "There's a reason why we put so much extra effort into the food. It's our way of raising money for Roger's school. All of us unattached ladies make up picnic baskets for the bachelors to bid on."

"The lucky bachelor has the honor of eating lunch with the maker of the basket he wins. Am I right?" Averil guessed.

"Indeed you are." Cecily took a sip of tea in an obvious attempt to keep from looking at him. "Of course, I'm looking forward to such a lovely event."

Averil didn't think twice about taking the hint. "Perhaps I might arrange to be there as well."

"If that would be agreeable to you."

"Most certainly." He had gone this far. Why not venture further? He cleared his throat. "If you are in need of an escort, perhaps you would consider me?"

"Indeed I would." She looked down upon the nearly empty dessert plate she held in her lap.

Averil could barely contain his delight. First, Cecily had

extended him an unexpected dinner invitation, and now this. He could hardly conceal his eagerness, although as a gentleman, he knew he must. "Are you sure your parents won't mind? After all, your mother didn't seem too pleased with me this afternoon when I soiled her rug."

Cecily giggled, although her mirth seemed a bit shaky. "She'll recover. And I'm sure Father won't mind."

Averil wasn't so sure, but he knew if he didn't seize the opportunity, he would lose any chance of seeing Cecily in the future. "All right. I'll go. In fact, I'd be delighted."

And why not? He had every intention of compensating them for the rug. And no one seemed to mind his presence at the dinner table.

Cecily took a bite of pie as her cheeks flushed pink. "Of course, you will mention our date to Father, won't you?" she asked after brushing the cloth napkin against her full, pink lips.

Averil swallowed. First, he had to make payment on the rug. Now, he had to ask permission to take Cecily to the Celebration of Spring event. He'd be packing his bags before sundown. "Certainly I'll mention it," he assured Cecily with more bravado than he felt.

In response, she averted her eyes to the last bit of apple pie remaining on her plate. A shy smile crossed her lips. Taking the risk would be worth it, after all. She rose from her seat. "I suppose we'd better take these things back inside."

Averil regretted seeing their time on the verandah come to an end. He set his plate, cup, and saucer on the tray. "Here. Let me help you with that."

He followed Cecily back into the house, down the hall, and into the dining room.

"An excellent meal once again, my dear," Mr. Eaton was saying to his wife.

"Thank you." She looked pleased with herself. Averil wondered why, since she had done little but rave throughout the meal about how she had the best cook in the city. It wasn't as though she had prepared the dinner herself. Yet, his mother always behaved in the same manner. He supposed that was the way of all women.

Hattie seemed to appear from out of nowhere to take the tray from Averil. His murmured thanks seemed to attract Mr. Eaton's notice.

"There you are, Mr. Kingsley. I suppose it's time for us to tend to our business." He sent Averil a knowing look, and then set his gaze in the direction of the foyer. The time of reckoning had arrived. Wordlessly, Cecily, her parents, and Averil proceeded to the area where the damage had been done. He was thankful the foyer was large.

"Where's the rug?" Averil asked. "Has it already been sent out for cleaning?"

"It's been hung out on the clothes line to dry," Mrs. Eaton said.

"Mr. Kingsley, would you mind showing me which electrical wall sconce you used to demonstrate your pneumatic carpet renovator?" Mr. Eaton asked.

Averil pointed to the one in question.

"That's what I thought." He nodded. "Mr. Kingsley, that sconce doesn't work properly. I'm sorry my wife and daughter weren't aware of that fact. If they had been, this whole unfortunate incident could have been avoided. That is why I won't hold you or the Capital Duster Company responsible for the fate of our rug."

Averil wanted to hear Mr. Eaton repeat the verdict, just in case he had misheard. "You won't?"

"No, I won't." He extended his hand to seal the agreement.

Accepting his hand, Averil felt as though the weight of the Capital Duster Model 1045 had been lifted from his shoulders. "So you mean to say that my pneumatic carpet renovator works just fine?"

Mr. Eaton chuckled. "I can't promise that, but I can promise you it almost certainly wouldn't have worked with this sconce."

Cecily rocked back and forth excitedly from heel to toe. "So you can buy a Capital Duster for Mother, after all?"

"I didn't say I wanted one yet," Mother said. Her doubtful words belied the pleading expression she sent her husband.

Mr. Eaton rubbed his chin. "I suppose, under the circumstances, I will allow you to demonstrate your machine."

"I'd be delighted, except I don't have it with me at the moment."

"That's understandable. Would you be willing to stop by on Monday morning?"

"Would I!" Averil realized he sounded like a schoolboy being offered a lollipop. He composed himself before he spoke again. "Yes, I would. Thank you for extending me another chance, Mr. Eaton."

"Certainly. I'm obliged to you, since our faulty sconce was partly to blame for the mishap."

Averil wanted to ask about the Celebration of Spring as he had promised Cecily, but he had the feeling he'd better not press his luck. Instead, he bid the family farewell. As soon as his feet hit the walk, he whistled a happy tune.

❧

"Augusta!" Cecily said excitedly to her sister the next morning. "Did you see the morning mail? There's a letter from Professor Tobias!" She crooked her finger, motioning Augusta to follow her into the kitchen.

"A letter? But he sees us every week. Why would he be writing to us?"

"I don't know," Cecily answered as they approached the kitchen table, where the mail had been left unattended. "It's addressed to Father."

Augusta lifted the letter in question out of the pile and studied it before handing it to Cecily. She took in a breath with such gusto that a one-note tune escaped her lips. "What do you think it's about?"

"I have no idea, but it looks as though he used formal writing paper. It must be important."

Augusta took Cecily by the hand and led her to the music room. "I can't wait until Father reads it!" Augusta nearly jumped with joy. "Maybe he's asking if he can court me! Wouldn't that be just wonderful?" In her excitement, Augusta sat at the piano and began playing a lively tune.

Cecily watched her sister's fingers move across the keys, stopping now and again when she stumbled over the notes. She wondered what her lovely sister saw in Professor Tobias. He seemed to cultivate his image with precision. Apparently he wanted the world to think of him as the careless intellectual. Often he arrived for their lessons without the proper sheets of music. While rummaging through a stack of papers to look for them, he could still manage to deliver a delightful biography of one of the masters of classical music.

A lock of blond hair was forever hanging loosely over his spectacles so that he was in constant need of swiping it away. His wardrobe appeared haphazard. Though always clean and with his shirt collars properly starched, the pieces did not always match well, and his suit coats had the look of garments whose owner economized by using them as pajamas. Nevertheless, if Professor Tobias was the man of her sister's dreams, Cecily wasn't about to discourage her. If she were to assess him with kindness in mind, Cecily supposed Professor Tobias offered a certain kind of charm, in his way.

"Yes, that would be wonderful, Augusta."

"Just think," Augusta said, "we will begin courting almost exactly the same day."

Suddenly chagrined, Cecily nervously twisted a loose strand of hair with her forefinger. "What do you mean?"

Augusta stopped playing. "Mr. Kingsley, of course! I overheard you invite him to the Celebration of Spring."

Cecily's forefinger immediately journeyed to the front of her puckered lips. "Shhh! No one is supposed to know that. Mother would be appalled if she knew I invited him. She wouldn't think it proper for a lady."

"Then I suppose a proper lady sits at home alone," Augusta noted. "He's new to the city. If you hadn't told him about the celebration, how would he have known about it?"

Cecily hadn't thought of that. "Father is bound to suspect something when Averil asks him about it."

"On a firstname basis, I see." Augusta's eyebrows shot up.

"Only in my mind. We really don't know each other at all."

Augusta put her hand on Cecily's shoulder. "Well, I wouldn't worry about Father suspecting anything. He'll never think twice about it." Augusta sighed. "I do so admire you, Cecily. I would never have the nerve to ask a man to escort me to the Celebration of Spring." She began playing once more.

"You wouldn't?" Doubt colored Cecily's voice. "Yet you have enough nerve to tighten your corset when it's time for Professor Tobias to give us a voice lesson."

Augusta straightened herself, then gave Cecily a sideways glance as she continued to play. "Do you think he notices?"

"I doubt he notices much of anything. But if that letter says what we think it does, then you've been successful in garnering his attention."

Their mother called from the kitchen. "Augusta! May we see you a moment?"

"Yes, Mother!" Augusta answered. She turned to Cecily. "I wonder if they've read the letter?"

"I'm sure that's why they want to see you."

"Come with me. I don't want you to miss this!" Augusta clasped her hands just underneath her chin and looked at the ceiling dreamily. "Imagine! Me, Augusta Eaton, one day being called Mrs. Osmond Tobias!" She let out an exaggerated sigh.

"Let's see how the courtship progresses first." Cecily laughed. When the girls reached the kitchen, neither of their parents looked happy. Father was lingering over a half-filled cup of coffee, and Mother was still nibbling on a slice of toasted bread. Usually this was a pleasant time for the elder Eatons. With their children pursuing their own weekend interests, the couple spent this time in solitude, renewing their relationship and relishing each other's company. For them to summon Augusta, or any of the children, was highly unusual. When she saw her father's sour expression, Cecily knew the letter's contents could not be good.

"We only called Augusta," Mother reminded them when she saw Cecily.

"I told her to come with me, Mother."

Father's eyebrows shot up. "So you were expecting some news?"

"Not especially." Augusta cast her gaze to the table as though she were taking great interest in the nearly empty pitcher of juice. Yet the Eaton children were never successful in keeping secrets from their parents. "Cecily did tell me that a letter from Os—Professor Tobias—arrived by post this morning."

"I see. And you think it contains good news?"

"I hope so." Augusta looked at Father with hopeful eyes.

"No doubt," Father observed. "Would you like to see what your instructor has to say, Augusta?"

As her younger sister nodded and took the letter from Father, Cecily clenched her teeth in worry. If Professor Tobias wanted to court Augusta, why would their father be so agitated? Cecily looked at Augusta as she read the letter to herself, hoping to see a glimmer of happiness on her face.

Instead, Augusta threw the letter on the floor and ran out of the room.

# four

What could Professor Tobias have written in his letter to vex Augusta so much? Cecily wondered. She could see how besotted her younger sister had become with the music teacher. She took special pains to look her best on music lesson day. An hour before the lesson was to begin, Augusta donned one of her best day dresses and then positioned herself in front of her vanity mirror. She assessed herself with care and then pinched her cheeks and bit her lips to bring the blood to the surface for color. Even though the result of such efforts was short-lived, Augusta didn't seem to mind punishing her poor face.

Cecily shuddered whenever she witnessed Augusta's actions. Her own cheeks looked nothing like fresh apples, nor did her lips resemble robust pink roses. Still, she couldn't imagine imposing such voluntary torture on her own features. Not for any man. Not even for Averil Kingsley.

Averil Kingsley! Whatever was she thinking?

She returned her thoughts to her sister and her strange music lesson day rituals. On every other day of the week, Augusta whooshed her hair into an indifferent bun, but Saturdays brought about quite a fuss. Each Friday evening, Augusta pored over Mother's ladies periodicals and studied pictures of new hair-styles. Then she would do her best to imitate them. The result was a muchimproved look. Cecily thought to suggest that her sister should style her hair with as much care every other day of the week, but thought better of it.

Cecily rooted for her sister, hoping Professor Tobias would recognize her efforts. While in Cecily's eyes, he wasn't the most attractive man on earth, apparently her sister saw him in a different light. Cecily shook her head as she recalled his features. Sparse blond hair and black-rimmed spectacles accentuating an anemic countenance did nothing to make Cecily swoon. Yet his presence pleased Augusta. Their parents couldn't object to his lineage, even though Cecily speculated that he could barely scratch out a living on the money he made from teaching music. Why, Professor Tobias should be honored that Augusta cared a whit about him. Augusta would have cherished a love letter, giggled over it, read it and reread it, kept it in a special, secret place. No, this was no message of love.

Then what was it?

Cecily rushed to retrieve the abandoned letter, but paused when she remembered propriety. "May I read the letter, Father?"

He hesitated. A sigh escaped his lips. "I suppose you may as well. You'll find out soon enough, anyway."

Cecily unfolded the plain white stationery. Professor Tobias's handwriting appeared as she expected it would, with perfectly formed, small letters:

*Dear Mr. Eaton,*

*This past Friday morning marked the second anniversary of the first day I began teaching your daughters the joys and challenges of performing song. Our lessons have been my privilege and pleasure.*

*Allow me to compliment your elder daughter. Miss Cecily's voice is a delight to the ears. Not only is she blessed with a wide range, but also she is successful in the execution of any song I present to her. I must say I am pleased with her continued accomplishment on the piano as well.*

*Miss Augusta is another matter. While she is a delightful girl, her lack of progress indicates that she fails to take her lessons, either in voice or piano, as seriously as Miss Cecily. I understand you are free to disagree with my assessment and seek to employ another instructor for her. However, unless Miss Augusta undertakes a dramatic increase in practice, she has reached the pinnacle of her*

accomplishment with the piano. Because of its limited range, I cannot anticipate that her voice will develop into one of an accomplished and talented singer. Please accept my assurances that if she
continues to keep in practice with the occasional song, Miss
Augusta should enjoy years of singing as a pleasurable enough pas-
time among close friends and family.

Because it is my belief that it is beyond my capabilities to impart
any additional knowledge or skill to Miss Augusta, with much
regret I have reached the unfortunate conclusion that for me to continue lessons with her would be an unwise use of your resources and
her talents, which might better be applied to the pleasurable and
ladylike skills of needlecraft or the arrangement of flowers. May
this letter serve as a formal dismissal of Miss Augusta.

However, it would be my great honor and pleasure to continue
instructing Miss Cecily. I expect to see her next Saturday.

Thank you for your indulgence and understanding.

Yours,
Osmond Tobias

Cecily gasped. "Father, no! Now I can understand why Augusta
is upset!"

"No wonder," he agreed. "Although I must admit, Augusta's
talents with song are limited." He winced.

"How heartless of Professor Tobias, all the same."

"I agree," Mother added.

Cecily placed the letter on the table. "I must console her. May I?"
He nodded. "Please do."

"It is quite distressing," Mother agreed. "Please, Cecily, see if
you can help."

"Yes, Mother." Without another moment's hesitation, Cecily
hurried up the stairs to her sister's room. She wasn't surprised to
see that the door was shut. She turned the knob and found it
was locked as well. She knocked. "Augusta?"

No answer.

"Augusta! I know you're there."

"Leave me alone. I don't want to talk to anybody. Especially you, Cecily." Icicles seemed to hang from her words.

Cecily half choked and then muttered, "That awful man! I'll never let him come between my sister and me!"

She stepped quickly to her own room and made her way to her vanity. She hadn't used her skeleton key in awhile, so it took a few moments to retrieve it from under several pairs of silk stockings. She rushed back to her sister's room and knocked again.

"Open the door," Cecily commanded. "This is your last chance."

"You are not my mother," Augusta answered. "I shall open the door when I'm good and ready."

"Very well then. I warned you." Cecily used her key to enter.

As soon as she saw her sister, she regretted her action. Augusta was lying in a heap on her bed, her beige cotton dress blending with the down comforter. Her face was buried in a pillow, which was partially concealed by unfettered blond locks. Augusta's slim frame shook with sobs.

Cecily strode over to Augusta's bed and knelt beside it. She placed a loving hand on her sister's shoulder.

Augusta turned her face in Cecily's direction. "How did you get in here?"

Cecily held up the key.

Augusta sneered and then buried her face back into the pillow. "I told you I don't want to see anybody," she mumbled into the cloth-covered goose down. "Especially not you."

"What did I do?" Cecily sat on the edge of the bed.

"Didn't you read the letter? He still wants to keep you. Apparently he thinks you're far superior to me in both voice and piano." Augusta broke out into fresh sobs.

"I'm no better than you are."

"That's a lie, and you know it," Augusta spat out. "Who needs a sister who steals a girl's beau?"

"Augusta, he is not your beau."

Augusta narrowed her eyes. "He would have been, if not for you."

"Really? Professor Tobias hasn't promenaded with you, eaten dinner at our house, or asked to court you," Cecily pointed out with as much gentleness as she could.

"Maybe not. But can't a girl dream?" Augusta sat upright and sniffled.

"Of course a girl can dream. What upsets me is that you think I would ever come between you and someone you wanted as a suitor. You know I would never do that."

Augusta blew her nose into the cotton handkerchief she had balled up in her fist. "I know." She sniffled. "I—I suppose you might be right." Her voice grew stronger. "Why, you must be right. It's plain to see he prefers you to me! How can he not? Obviously, he finds your singing and playing much more elegant than mine could ever be!" Augusta's sobs began anew. She laid her face in her open hands.

Cecily sat beside her sister and placed a consoling arm around her shaking shoulders. Trying to argue logic with Augusta in her state of heightened emotion would be folly indeed, but she had to say something to console her. "Don't be silly," she whispered.

"It's true!" Augusta pushed Cecily's arm away. "He still wants to teach you music. What am I supposed to do on lesson day now? Sit in my room and listen while you sing him love songs?"

"Love songs? Now I know you're mad!" Cecily laughed at the mere thought.

"It's not funny!" Augusta crossed her arms.

"I know it isn't. I just can't imagine—" Cecily couldn't contain a fresh wave of giggles.

"I see. You don't think Professor Tobias is the least bit handsome, or charming, or witty, or. . .or anything!"

"He isn't worth defending." Cecily rose to her feet.

"Isn't worth defending! The love of my life isn't worth defending? How can you say that?"

Cecily sighed. No answer she could think up would be acceptable to Augusta when she was in such a state.

"Well?" Augusta prodded.

"I'm sure he has his good points, but I promise you, I have no interest in Professor Tobias beyond what he can teach me in music." Cecily raised an eyebrow. "And come to think of it, the only reason I take music lessons is to sing and play a little for our friends."

"Apparently he doesn't seem to think I'm even talented enough for that."

"I'm sure he doesn't mean it like that."

"Maybe not, but no matter how you read what he wrote in his letter, he still thinks you're much more talented than I am."

"No, he doesn't." Cecily realized her weak argument would not convince anyone. She had a thought. "But he thinks quite highly of you. He said so. He even said you are a 'delightful girl.'" Cecily felt an inner surge of triumph swell in her chest.

"Why don't you just quote the letter outright? Obviously you've memorized every word," Augusta hissed.

Cecily's perceived victory dissolved, leaving her feeling empty except for a feeling of resentment toward the music instructor for being the cause of strife between herself and her sister. "No. No, I haven't."

"Not that I blame you," Augusta retorted, her words showing all too well that she had ceased to listen. "What girl wouldn't like such compliments?"

Cecily shook her head and tried to make Augusta understand. "I don't enjoy any so-called compliment that comes at the expense of my sister's happiness."

Augusta pouted.

Cecily took her sister's hands, still moist from tears, in her own. "Say, why don't I tell Father I won't be taking lessons anymore?" As soon as she uttered the words, Cecily regretted them. She needed coaching on a few of the difficult notes on the hymn she wanted to sing as a solo in church the following week. Without her teacher's help, she'd never get over the rough spots.

"You won't?" Augusta looked into Cecily's eyes. Her face shone like the morning sun. "You mean, you'll stop taking lessons altogether?"

Cecily swallowed. Either Augusta had forgotten about Cecily's solo and how nervous she felt about it, or she was simply pretending the next week had slipped her mind. She stalled, hoping Augusta would let her take back her impromptu offer. "I would have to think of something to say to Father. He'll be disappointed."

"Do you really think he cares one way or the other whether we take music?" Augusta let go of Cecily's hands and rose from the bed. She looked out the window, but her face was blank, as though she didn't see anything. "Perhaps he would look at our discontinuation as one less worry and expense."

"I don't think he sees it that way." Cecily watched Augusta to see if she would relent, but she did not. Cecily could see she needed heavy artillery. "You know how much church means to Father. Why, he would be mightily vexed if we didn't sing solos and duets on Sundays anymore."

Augusta turned to Cecily. "What do you mean?"

"Without Professor Tobias to help us practice, how do you think we can keep singing?"

Augusta placed her hands on her hips. "Surely your confidence isn't that weak, Cecily. You've been taking lessons for two years. Why, I'm sure you could sing the entire hymnbook in your sleep, if you had half a mind to."

"I doubt that."

Augusta sat down at her vanity and began rearranging her comb and brush, even though their order was acceptable by any standard.

Cecily sighed. Augusta was deliberately ignoring all reason. How could she change her mind now? She stood up as though the motion would give her strength. "I suppose I can let Father down easily, somehow. And they'll just have to do without me at the next recital, that's all." She tried not to wince. Cecily had been practicing a difficult piano sonata for months in hopes of pleasing her parents with a fantastic performance in the annual music recital in June. She visualized herself deteriorating from a show of harmonious notes to the sounds of a toddler's first attempts at hitting the ivories.

Obviously unaware of Cecily's inner turmoil, Augusta jumped from her seat, reminding Cecily of a little girl on Christmas morning. "Thank you, Cecily!" She embraced her sister. "If I had to sit all alone, listening to you sing and play for Professor Tobias, why, I couldn't bear it. I just couldn't bear it."

Cecily broke the embrace and sent Augusta what she hoped was a smile that didn't betray her regret. Her sister was worth the sacrifice, wasn't she?

⁂

Averil slid into a pew near the front of the small church, a building of gray stone that was the closest place of worship within walking distance of his boardinghouse. He had passed it at least ten times during the past week. Observing the sign stating the church's name and denomination, the pastor's name, and the appointed hours of Sunday school and worship, he had made a mental note to attend services that weekend. In fact, he was earlier than the nine o'clock hour for worship, giving him plenty of time to select a seat.

The church interior appeared as he expected. Dark burnished wood abounded. He found the darkness comforting, reminding him of his home church.

"Sit up front every Sunday, Son," Father always said. "Let everyone see you at church. It's good for business."

Wherever he happened to be, Averil attended church, but not for the reasons his father suggested. Though a Christian and a moral man, the senior Kingsley seemed to lack the fire and conviction Averil felt. Yet Father saw to it that his children never missed a service. For that, Averil would be eternally grateful.

A creature of habit, he favored sitting on the far, left-hand side of any place of worship. Ignoring the right, he searched among the remaining polished mahogany pews for an empty place. The front had a few spots, but he wasn't ready to be that conspicuous in his attendance. The second was full, but the third pew was nearly empty. He made his way up the left-side aisle and took a place at the end of the pew. Additional worshipers were pouring in by this time. Some chatted among themselves, while others meditated.

Eager to observe his new surroundings, Averil studied the stained-glass windows. The one he sat beside, a formidable and colorful work of art, pictured John the Baptist baptizing the Lord Jesus in the river, with the dove of the Holy Spirit hovering over both men. A brass plaque proclaimed, "In Memory of Roger Swathmore, from his loving wife, Matilda."

Each side of the sanctuary had four stainedglass windows. Each one depicted a well-loved Bible scene. He was sitting too close to the front to see them all, but he viewed those within his peripheral range with wonder: Jesus with the children, Moses on Mount Sinai, the women at the empty tomb. Each window brought the scenes to life. Ostensibly, every window was donated in memory of a deceased loved one. Averil couldn't see well enough to read all of the brass plaques.

Having taken in his surroundings, Averil thought that if the service lived up to its setting, this little church might be his home for worship until he left Richmond. He let out a satisfied sigh and opened his Bible. He would read Psalms as he waited for the service to begin.

Averil's relative solitude proved to be short-lived. Soon the pleasant scent of gardenia and the rustle of a Sunday dress interrupted his reading. He cut his gaze to the right and saw none other than Miss Cecily Eaton.

Cecily!

She was walking toward him, ready to sit beside him right on the same pew! He scooted over to the left so that the side of his arm touched the end. Although he tried to act as though Cecily's unexpected appearance had no effect on him whatsoever, he let out a shaky breath.

The day he first saw the regal young woman, when she opened the door to him so he could demonstrate his pneumatic carpet renovator, he had thought her the most beautiful being on the face of the earth. Today she appeared even more ravishing. The hat she wore was a large pink affair, covered with white-and-pink roses on its brim. Wisps of light brown hair hung near her heart-shaped face, framing perfect brown eyes flecked with gold, cheeks the color of newly blossomed pink rose petals, and skin as white as fresh cream. The pink dress she wore suited her and the spring day well. The vision of her left him feeling awestruck.

"Miss. . .Miss Eaton," he managed to stutter. "Good morning."

"Good morning," she answered.

Did averted eyes mean she suffered a sudden attack of shyness? Or was she simply acting the part of a lady? Politeness dictated that he not meditate upon his speculations too long.

"Mrs. Eaton. Miss Eaton." He nodded to Cecily's sister. What was her name? He couldn't recall.

"Good day," the younger Miss Eaton answered, while her mother sent him a chilly nod.

"Mr. Eaton." Averil nodded.

"Mr. Kingsley," Mr. Eaton responded with a smile. Averil felt a surge of relief when he noted the warmth in his tone. "I had no idea you were attending our church."

"This is my first time here."

"And you sat in our pew?" Mrs. Eaton's eyebrows shot up.

Averil felt a flush of embarrassment. Did she think he had made a deliberate attempt to sit beside her family? He gave himself a swift mental kick for not reading the nameplate on the back of the pew. He knew the custom well. The family that donated a pew sat there forevermore.

"I did not think to read the nameplate beforehand, but I am delighted by this coincidence," Averil said without the slightest bit of exaggeration.

"As are we," Cecily assured him.

Averil tried not to smile from ear to ear. Perhaps Cecily was just being polite, displaying the impeccable manners with which she was bred.

"Will you be attending Sunday school class after the service, Mr. Kingsley?" Cecily asked.

"Why, yes, I was thinking about it."

"Don't just think about it. Come to my class with me." Her eyes sparkled.

"They. . .I mean, the others in your class, they won't mind?" He knew his voice sounded too eager, but he couldn't contain himself.

"Of course not. Why would they mind?" she asked. "We always welcome new people."

"Or," suggested Mrs. Eaton, "you might consider one of the other classes. I do believe the gentlemen's class is discussing stewardship."

"Stewardship." Did she think he was a poor steward? Or was Mrs. Eaton just hoping he would take the hint and find his way to another class, away from her elder daughter? He decided on a noncommittal answer. "A fine topic indeed, Mrs. Eaton."

Mrs. Eaton sent him a satisfied nod. "A topic any one of us would do well to investigate."

"You are most welcome to join us, Mr. Kingsley," Augusta piped up, "but you probably wouldn't like our Young Misses' class. We're talking about 'How to be a Beautiful Woman.'"

"Somehow I doubt that subject would apply to Mr. Kingsley," Cecily pointed out.

"Thank you for your vote of confidence on that matter." Averil was pleased when his feeble attempt at humor was rewarded by Cecily's delightful giggle.

Cecily's look of encouragement, which seemed to override her mother's message, pleased him even more. "Mrs. Jones promised us we'd talk about the merits of virtue in connection with new-fangled moving pictures."

"One cannot be too virtuous in this day and age," Mrs. Eaton said.

"Yes. The new century upon us brings so much promise and so much temptation." He wished he hadn't used the word "temptation." Cecily was sitting much too close. The scent of gardenia on any other woman would have seemed ordinary, but on Cecily it seemed like none other than the aroma of heaven itself. Self-conscious, Averil shifted away from her, but not enough as to appear rude, he hoped.

"Indeed, there is so much temptation today," Mrs. Eaton agreed. "A virtuous young man must do everything he can to avoid even a whiff of scandal. Especially if he is to succeed in business." She looked down her nose at him.

"My father would agree with you most heartily, Madame." Averil hoped the mention of his father would provide him with the proper opening to give them more information about his roots—namely, that Averil Kingsley Sr. owned the Capital Duster Company. Perhaps then, she might not be as disdainful of Averil's presence in Cecily's class.

"Indeed. I'm sure your father is a fine man." Mrs. Eaton opened her Bible and began reading.

"He must be, to have reared such a levelheaded young man as you are," Mr. Eaton interjected.

Averil sent him a grateful smile. Perhaps Cecily's father wasn't as adverse to him attending his daughter's class as his wife seemed to be.

Averil had no intention of pressing his attentions upon any

young woman whose mother seemed opposed to such a relationship. Yet when Cecily shared the hymnbook with him, leaning just a bit more closely than necessary, suddenly her mother's opinion didn't seem to matter.

# five

Just before Mrs. Watson struck the first notes on the pipe organ, Cecily fought the urge to invite Averil to her class once more. She had already been too forward, and Mother's admonishing looks sent in her direction didn't ease her guilt. Surely Mother was thinking of nothing but Delmar Williams, the man she had selected for Cecily.

Cecily could read her mother's mind. Mother was wondering how Delmar would feel if he knew Cecily shared a hymnal with another man. Well, Mother would just have to wonder. At that moment, Cecily didn't care.

A chill ran up her spine. She didn't usually act this way around men. What had come over her?

Cecily didn't have to give Averil a second glance to know exactly what had come over her. In spite of the adventure with his machine and Mother's rug, in spite of his being at least a head shorter than she was, in spite of Mother's hopes for a match with Delmar, in spite of the fact that Averil's position as a door-to-door salesman would not meet Mother's standards—in spite of all this, Cecily's heart went flitter-flutter when he was near.

What was it about Averil Kingsley, purveyor of the Capital Duster Electric Pneumatic Carpet Renovator? Certainly his sparkling eyes and pleasing personality attracted her, but there was something more, an indescribable element that made her want to draw closer. Indescribable or not, she wanted to be near him, to find out more about him.

"You've chosen a wonderful day to join us," Father whispered to Averil.

Cecily sent her father a grateful smile. At least someone in her family welcomed Averil.

Father's grin grew broad. "Our very own Cecily will be singing a solo."

Averil took in an audible breath. "I did choose a great day to worship in this sanctuary!" He turned his attention to Cecily. "I shall look forward to hearing you, Miss Cecily."

*Oh, no!*

Cecily's heart throbbed. In her excitement of seeing Averil again, then her dismay upon remembering Delmar, she had forgotten all about her solo! Averil had never heard her sing. What would he think? How she wished she hadn't agreed to stop taking music lessons with Professor Tobias! If only she had practiced with him at least through the end of the week. She was shaky on the high note, and now she would have to sing with Averil in the congregation. If only she hadn't let Professor Tobias talk her into trying a challenging song, a song that might be easy for a professional singer but with a scale that hit the top of her limited range. Oh, foolish pride, the force that convinced her to take on more than she could handle with ease. She prayed that the Lord would overlook her madness and somehow let her get through her hymn without a mistake.

Cecily worked herself into such frenzy that she barely heard the announcements and opening prayer. Her solo was slated to follow the offering. Normally she enjoyed listening to the organ solo, but this time she blocked out the music and rehearsed her own song in her mind. She closed her eyes and pictured herself delivering the song without missing a single note. Perhaps that would work.

Augusta's reassuring hand pressed hers. Cecily opened her eyes to see her sister nodding in approval. So Augusta thought she was praying. Pangs of guilt assailed her. If her sister knew her real thoughts, she wouldn't be so admiring. Cecily felt more ashamed than ever.

"And now we shall have the pleasure of hearing a wonderful hymn as sung by Miss Cecily Eaton," Pastor Richards announced all too soon. "The song she has selected today is one of my all-time favorites, 'All Hail the Power of Jesus' Name.'"

Cecily swallowed. She nodded to Averil, who, like the gentleman he was, rose from his seat to allow her to pass. He wore a look of anticipation meant to be heartening, she was certain. Instead, his unspoken support served to make her more nervous.

She walked up to the front of the hushed sanctuary, self-consciously holding her shoulders back and tilting her head high. Once she had taken her position in front of the communion rail, Cecily swept her gaze over the congregants, most of whom she had known all her life. Smiles of reassurance calmed her. She made a point not to meet Averil's stare. Surely his rapt expression would hold much more anticipation than she could bear.

The pastor wasn't finished. "Yes, my friends. As the song says, 'Bring forth the royal diadem, and crown Him Lord of all.' Today, I ask, what are you doing to show the world that Jesus is king of your life? As Miss Cecily sings to us, let us hear her words and meditate upon this sound wisdom—" He stopped and grinned so the congregation would recognize the pun.

The congregation granted him an obligatory chuckle.

He continued. "Let us all remember this wisdom as we listen to the melodic harmony of our very own Miss Cecily Eaton." He stepped down from the pulpit and headed for a seat in the front pew, all the while casting a look of encouragement in her direction.

Cecily knew how much her friends anticipated her song. She remembered the first time she sang solo in church, when she was a child of eight. Even then, her slightly off-key rendition of "Oh for a Thousand Tongues" met with a great many compliments and much encouragement afterward.

At that time, she had needed the praise. Cecily had expected the whole church to erupt in applause for her song, but they remained silent after the last organ note echoed into stillness. She tried not to pout or cry as she made her way back to the pew where she and her family always sat. Only afterward did Mother explain that no one ever clapped in church, not even for a presentation as outstanding as hers. Now that she was grown, Cecily could appreciate the awesome peace that followed solos. She had learned that the silent reverence and appreciation of a performance given for the Lord surpassed any human accolades.

*Please, Lord, help me to honor Thee with my performance.*

She nodded to Mrs. Watson, the organist. As they had rehearsed, the older woman hit the first note with her usual flair. Hearing the familiar introduction eased Cecily's mind. She concentrated on her breathing. Her voice grew stronger. Through the next stanzas, she relaxed, remembering to breathe the way Professor Tobias had instructed.

Cecily almost started the last stanza too soon, when she remembered that during rehearsals Mrs. Watson mentioned she planned to expand the bridge. The organist always enjoyed playing for soloists since she could embellish and add music between verses, a practice she wasn't permitted when playing for congregational singing. Cecily clapped her mouth shut and hoped no one noticed her near error. Suddenly, Mrs. Watson broke into the chorus where Cecily should have resumed singing. After missing her cue, Cecily froze. Mrs. Watson continued with the first line, then nodded toward Cecily. She felt her face turn a hundred shades of red.

She glanced at the congregants to see if anyone noticed her mistake. Judging from their expressions, they hadn't. Except for Augusta. She knew how long and hard Cecily worked on each solo, enough to have memorized each line herself. Augusta gave her a nod of encouragement, which made her feel well enough to keep going.

Through her peripheral vision, Cecily could see that Mrs. Watson was in fine form, swaying back and forth as she played. Her confidence inspired Cecily to glance at Averil. His chin was tilted upward, and his eyes caught the light. He even leaned forward slightly, as though he didn't want to miss a single inflection.

Just as their gazes met, Cecily felt a lump in the back of her throat. She felt a sudden urge to cough.

*No! Not now!*

Cecily managed a few more notes before she felt tightness in her chest and then a sudden catch in her throat. The high note was only two beats away. *Oh, no! I'm not going to make it!*

Why hadn't she stayed with Professor Tobias? Why had she let Mrs. Watson talk her into a higher key for the last verse?

*I wanted to show off, and now I'm going to embarrass myself, right in front of everybody I ever cared anything about.*

Her silent prayer was too late. Cecily's voice cracked, right on the most important word, "Lord." Ever the poised performer, she recovered quickly, but not quickly enough. She glanced at the third pew. Everyone cringed—including Averil. Humiliated, she didn't dare look elsewhere.

Somehow she finished the last bars of her song and bowed her head in a mixture of reverence and shame. Just as quickly, she looked up just in time to see Averil stand up and clap. The claps came in rapid succession, reverberating throughout the sanctuary. She watched, mouth open, as Augusta stood and clapped too, soon joined by her parents. Clusters of friends and neighbors rose and joined in, until finally the entire church delivered Cecily a standing ovation.

She stood for a moment and gawked at the congregation. Clapping was unheard of in her church. Some even disapproved of the idea of a worldly show of approval for any song or performance meant to honor the Lord, which Cecily had certainly meant to do with her song. But on that day, her friends and family made an exception for her. Even old Mrs. Roarke, too infirm to stand, clapped as she remained seated in her usual place on the far right side of a back pew.

Had Cecily not been in a state of shock, she might have stood in front of everyone and bawled. Instead, she gathered her wits and hurried back to her seat. Despite everyone's enthusiastic approval, especially Averil's, she felt chagrined. She didn't deserve their applause, and she knew it. Now Averil was sure to think she made a habit of singing poorly. Then again, would she have developed a catch in her throat if Averil hadn't been present?

Only Augusta's consoling pats on her hand kept Cecily from bursting into tears. She couldn't do that. And to depart in the middle of worship because of wounded pride would be even worse than to break out in sobs.

Cecily didn't look at anyone for the rest of the service. She wanted to concentrate on the pastor's message, but after his glowing introduction of her solo, Cecily could only stare over the top of his head, at the corner of the ceiling. To her shame, afterward she realized that she couldn't remember a word of the sermon. She couldn't recall a time when she had been so eager to see a worship service end.

Then she remembered. She had invited Averil to her class! Maybe he forgot.

As soon as the benediction concluded, Averil turned to her. "If the invitation to join your class is still open, I'd be honored to attend."

"Really?" Did he truly want to be seen with her after such a blunder, or was he just being nice? "Are you quite certain?"

"But of course." He looked her straight in the eye. "Who wouldn't want to be seen with the church's star performer?"

She groaned and looked at the burnished wood floor. "You saw the worst performance of my life."

"All the reason for me to return to worship here," he said.

"One day in the near future, I want to see the best performance of your life too."

Cecily was so grateful for his kindness that she chuckled. How could just a few words from a stranger make her feel so warm inside? She didn't have time to contemplate her feelings. The older people were starting to settle in the sanctuary for their class, which meant everyone under thirty had to vacate to the classrooms.

Cecily led Averil along a narrow hallway and down a rickety flight of steps. "Careful. This church was built just after the War Between the States. I'm afraid it is not up to our modern standards."

"Perhaps the corridors wouldn't be so narrow had hoop skirts still been the style after the war," Averil quipped.

Cecily laughed at his mindless banter. A little humor was just what she needed. After they cleared the last step, Averil joined her, walking by her side. Having him close felt good.

"I understand your class will be talking about moving pictures," he observed.

"Yes. We've been studying newfangled inventions. Today the question is, 'Moving Pictures: Are They Good or Evil?'"

Averil's dark eyebrows shot up. "Sounds like a subject sure to spark vigorous debate."

"Undoubtedly." Cecily rolled her eyes toward him. "Maybe next week you can talk about electric pneumatic carpet renovators."

He chuckled. "I may be eager to sell my product, but not that eager. I don't engage in commerce on Sunday. Of course, any other day of the week, I'd be delighted to talk about my carpet renovators." His smile disarmed her.

Cecily smiled back and then led him through the door to the class. She kept her gaze concentrated on the knotted pine floors. Even though she knew her friends wouldn't allude to her mishap during the solo, she was still too upset about her error to talk to them. She just wanted the class to end so she could go home.

As Cecily had predicted, the class delighted in meeting Averil. His quick wit helped to keep the discussion lively. She found her thoughts drifting away from the lesson and focusing on his insights.

"What do you think, Miss Eaton?"

"Think about what?"

The class giggled, causing Cecily fresh embarrassment.

Mrs. Jones adjusted her spectacles as she studied Cecily. "Do you agree with Mr. Hanes's assertion that all moving pictures are evil?"

"I've given it some thought," Cecily stalled. "I believe that any medium can be used for good or evil."

"But so many moving pictures are evil!" Mr. Hanes—better known to Cecily as Matthew—protested. "The shocking things they portray in these moving pictures! Why, I don't dare speak of them in mixed company."

Mrs. Jones eyed him. "And how did you happen to become so well acquainted with these shocking pictures, Mr. Hanes?"

He squirmed. "Uh, a friend told me."

"I see," Mrs. Jones responded. "Well now, I don't expect you to go into detail, Mr. Hanes. Let us hear what Miss Eaton has to say."

"What comes from the mind all depends on the author," Cecily countered. "A person with evil intent will produce evil material, whether it be books, plays, or moving pictures. A person who is close to God wouldn't. He would make something that pleases the Lord." She opened her Bible and turned to Romans 8:8. "I looked up this verse last night when I was thinking about today's lesson. 'So then they that are in the flesh cannot please God.'"

"Very good, Miss Eaton. Your study of the Word serves you well."

"Thank you," Cecily muttered. She sent her gaze to the bare floor, unwilling to display how Mrs. Jones's praise pleased her. Perhaps now she could look her classmates in the eye once more.

She snuck a furtive glance at Averil and wondered if she should invite him to Sunday dinner. No. That would be too brazen. She would just have to wait, that's all.

≈

The next day, Averil swept the pneumatic carpet renovator across Mrs. Eaton's rug one last time and turned off the machine. The results pleased him.

"Why," said Mrs. Eaton, "I can't believe it! Every last piece of dirt came right up!"

"Naturally." Averil grinned so widely that his face hurt. Now he knew that with the proper electrical connection, his carpet renovator would work splendidly. Of course if it had failed and Mrs. Eaton had decided to tell all of Richmond, the Capital Duster Company wouldn't sell so much as its first unit in the city, and he'd have to peddle it elsewhere. Even worse, if he had to leave the city, he would no longer have reason to see Cecily.

"See, Mother?" Cecily said. "I told you that Mr. Kingsley's machine would work."

He glanced up at Cecily. His heart pounded as he drank in her beauty in a reaction that had become familiar. Her simple blue dress was hardly as elaborate as her Sunday dress had been, but that didn't matter. Cecily looked ravishing whether she appeared in a housedress or, he imagined, the most stunning ball gown.

To his delight, she sent him a sweet smile. He wished she had invited him to Sunday dinner after church the previous day. He wondered why she hadn't. Then he remembered Mrs. Eaton's unenthusiastic demeanor in his presence.

"I do believe you have proven yourself after all, Mr. Kingsley," Mrs. Eaton told him.

"There was no effort on my part," Averil answered. "The Capital Duster always proves itself, Mrs. Eaton."

Mrs. Eaton surveyed the machine. "In that case, I think I shall buy one, after all."

"You will?" Averil blurted out, then smiled. "Of course you

will." He gestured toward the machine. "What woman can resist the fine workmanship and convenience of this wondrous pneumatic carpet renovator?"

"Yes, indeed," Cecily agreed.

Mrs. Eaton studied the appliance. "And please include a set of accessories."

"Indeed I shall!" Averil whipped his receipt pad out of his vest pocket and began writing the order. "Standard or deluxe?"

"Standard," Mrs. Eaton answered.

"Standard it is, then." Averil nodded as he wrote. "There is one little thing," Mrs. Eaton interrupted as he concluded his calculations. "I don't keep so much money in the house, and Mr. Eaton isn't home at the moment to write a bank draft."

Averil nodded. The dilemma occurred often. "Don't worry, Mrs. Eaton. I'll be glad to stop by this evening, when Mr. Eaton is home."

Mrs. Eaton smiled. "That would be quite convenient. Thank you." Her last words were said over the gonging of a hall clock.

"Noon? Is it lunchtime already?" Cecily asked her mother. "Perhaps we might offer Mr. Kingsley a bite to eat."

Averil's heart returned to its rapid beating. So Cecily invited him to lunch! Perhaps she wasn't so averse to his company after all. "Why, thank you, I—"

"Isn't my daughter ever so polite?" Mrs. Eaton interjected. "She doesn't mind whom we invite to lunch. Anyone from the pastor to a door-to-door salesman."

"Oh." Averil was taken aback. "Why, uh, yes, Miss Eaton is the epitome of politeness and fine breeding." Averil plastered a smile on his face and did his best to ignore the sting of her mother's remark, even though its bite took the joy from making a sale. He let the insincere expression melt from his face. "I must be getting on my way. I appreciate your business, Mrs. Eaton, but I did lose Mrs. MacGregor's sale last week, so time is of the essence for me."

"You lost a sale?" Cecily's mouth dropped open. "But why?"

"I'm afraid I'm to blame. After the disaster with the rug, I told her these machines don't work." Mrs. Eaton pursed her lips in apology. "And I must admit that I'm sorry."

"Mother!" Cecily exclaimed. "Do you really think that an apology is enough? After all, Mr. Kingsley's livelihood is at stake. And what about his company's reputation?"

"I'll tell Mrs. MacGregor about my mistake. Sometime," Mrs. Eaton promised.

Averil tried not to let his face reveal his doubt. He suspected Mrs. Eaton was a proud woman. To admit a mistake to a neighbor whom she obviously considered an archrival would be the last thing she'd want to do. He wondered when the next train would be leaving for somewhere else. Maybe Danville.

Cecily broke in with a protest. "But, Mother, our family has taken food from Mr. Kingsley's mouth. We must make amends."

"But how?"

"Do let me walk over to Mrs. MacGregor's with Mr. Kingsley," Cecily suggested. "I'm certain I can help him explain everything to her."

Mother tilted her head in the direction of the kitchen. "But what about lunch?"

"You go ahead and eat. Mr. Kingsley and I will join you shortly. We'll be back as soon as we get everything straight with Mrs. MacGregor."

"But I don't know if the two of you walking together, unchaperoned, would be proper," Mrs. Eaton protested. "Pardon me, Mr. Kingsley, but we have only made your acquaintance for a very short time."

"Perhaps, but we would still be doing nothing improper," Cecily answered. "Mr. Kingsley and I will be walking less than a block in broad daylight. And I promise to come right back, as soon as we speak to her." Seeing Cecily's eyes widen and her hands clasped in front of her chest, Averil hoped Cecily's mother would give in. He knew he would never be able to resist such pleading.

"All right," Mrs. Eaton agreed. "I suppose since it's my fault that he lost his sale, the least I can do is let you help make amends."

"Thank you, Mother dear." Cecily kissed her mother on the cheek. "Mr. Kingsley, just let me get my hat. I want to look my best, you know. The reputation of the Capital Duster Electric Pneumatic Carpet Renovator is at stake!"

# six

"Good morning, Cecily." Mrs. MacGregor wrinkled her nose at Averil as though a skunk had entered her presence. "Good morning, Mr. Kingsley."

He tipped his hat. "Morning, Ma'am."

"I must say, I'm shocked that you're still here in the city," Mrs. MacGregor told him. "After the disaster on Friday, I can't imagine that anyone would want to buy what you're selling." She then concentrated her stare upon Cecily. "As for you, Cecily, I'm surprised. Why in the world are you standing right here on my front porch with this so-called salesman? Does your mother have any idea?"

"Yes, Ma'am. She knows all about it," Cecily answered. "I'm here to defend a fine product, the wonderful Capital Duster Electric Pneumatic Carpet Renovator."

The neighbor let out a hearty laugh. "Is that so? Your mother doesn't seem to think it's so wonderful. She told me it ruined her best rug. After that, I could never agree to buy one. Never." She sniffed. "I daresay my rugs are even more valuable than your mother's."

"Well." Cecily wanted to defend her mother's fine rugs, but decided that to argue the point wouldn't help her case. "It's true that Mother believed her rug to be ruined, and that's why she didn't speak favorably about the carpet renovator."

"Don't I know it." The neighbor bored her stare into Cecily.

Averil cleared his throat. "We are here, Madame, to tell you that after seeing the Capital Duster Electric Pneumatic Carpet Renovator in its true light, she has changed her mind."

"Oh?" Mrs. MacGregor folded her arms and kept her attention on Cecily. "I'm listening."

Cecily ignored her doubting posture. "You wouldn't believe it, Mrs. MacGregor. All the dirt on Mother's carpet this morning just vanished." She snapped her fingers. "It all disappeared right away when Mr. Kingsley used this wonderful machine on it. I wouldn't have believed it myself had I not witnessed it with my own eyes."

"I saw that rug and the state it was in. Your mother was nearly in tears about it," Mrs. MacGregor observed. "I never would have thought any carpet renovator would have touched it."

"Neither did we. We were sure it was a total loss," Cecily agreed.

Mrs. MacGregor leaned against the door. "So you say the dirt vanished in an instant? All of it?"

"Every last speck." Cecily nodded. "And that's why Mother bought her very own Capital Duster Electric Pneumatic Carpet Renovator."

Mrs. MacGregor cast a look down her long nose. "She did? Really?"

"Really."

"Miss Eaton is right," Averil interjected. "As soon as Mrs. Eaton saw how hygienic her home would become with continuous use of this fine machine, she was eager to purchase one for herself. I just wish you had been there to witness it, Mrs. MacGregor. Every last speck was gone in the blink of an eye." He snapped his fingers to illustrate. "And, Mrs. MacGregor, if you'll reconsider and place an order with me today, you too will find that the Capital Duster Electric Pneumatic Carpet Renovator performs in the same exemplary manner with each and every use."

"Well." Mrs. MacGregor unfolded her arms. "I have been considering buying a new machine for some time. Mine is getting a little bit of age on it." She touched her thumb and forefinger to her long chin.

"And I might add, Mrs. Eaton bought a fine set of accessories as well," Averil said. "I assure you, with such a fine device and easy-to-use accessories, the Eatons will enjoy one of the most sanitary houses in the city."

"Yes," Mrs. MacGregor responded in a tone that indicated she still wasn't convinced. She set her gaze once again upon Cecily. "My dear, you have been my neighbor for your entire life. I remember the day you came into this world just as surely as I remember the birth of my own daughter. So I expect you to tell me the truth. Are you saying he used the same machine on the rug? Or did he use a new one?"

"He used the very same one."

"Yes, indeed," Averil said.

"Indeed?" Mrs. MacGregor asked.

Cecily nodded. "You see, the carpet renovator worked all along. It only left dirt on the rug the first time because, well, because it was all my fault." Cecily cringed. "It seems I let Mr. Kingsley use an electrical outlet that wasn't working properly. Once the right amount of current went through the machine, it worked wonders."

"So your mother let an outlet go bad, eh? I'm surprised." A victorious smile slid over her mouth as she rubbed her chin. "All right, then. I'll reinstate my order."

"You will?" Averil asked. "Why, of course you will. Thank you, Mrs. MacGregor. I'm so pleased we managed to clear up this misunderstanding."

"Don't thank me. Thank Cecily." Mrs. MacGregor didn't wait for an answer. "Cecily, you say your mother ordered a set of accessories?"

"Yes, Ma'am."

"Standard," Averil elaborated.

"In that case," Mrs. MacGregor said, "put me down for a set of deluxe accessories."

Averil nodded and made the entry in his receipt book. "A very wise choice indeed, Mrs. MacGregor."

"I think so. As they say, you get what you pay for." Mrs.

MacGregor sent them a decisive nod. "You may come by this evening and pick up the bank draft from Mr. MacGregor."

"Yes, Ma'am." Averil tipped his hat. "Thank you, Ma'am. I know you will enjoy your new carpet renovator for many, many more years to come."

"Yes." Mrs. MacGregor smiled at Cecily. "Remember me to your mother."

"I will. And thank you."

Averil and Cecily exchanged victorious looks before Mrs. MacGregor could shut the front door. They turned and nearly glided down the brick walkway together.

"Two sales in one hour and both with accessories!" Averil exclaimed, beaming. "Now no one can tell me I'm not a good salesman."

"Is someone telling you that?"

His face clouded, but he didn't speak.

Cecily wished she hadn't let her curiosity get the better of her. She wondered who would try to undermine Averil's confidence. His boss, perhaps? Or a family member? Judging from his expression, he was in no mood to share his thoughts. "I'm sorry."

He brightened. "No, there's no need for you to be sorry."

"It's just that you. . .well. . ." She watched her boot-clad feet clomp, one in front of the other, as though she were a toddler who needed to observe them to keep from falling. "You exude such confidence. I never thought you'd doubt yourself for a moment." Then, remembering what Mother had told her about male pride, she wished she hadn't posed an idea that might corner him into confessing a weakness. " 'For verily I say unto you, That whosoever shall say unto this mountain, Be thou removed, and be thou cast into the sea; and shall not doubt in his heart, but shall believe that those things which he saith shall come to pass; he shall have whatsoever he saith.' "

"You have just quoted one of my favorite passages from the Book of Mark," Averil said, "one I have referred to time and time again in the course of my life."

"As have I." Trying to make light of the matter, she added, "As you can tell, since I have committed it to memory."

Their shared mirth broke the tension Cecily had become aware of since she brought up the subject of doubt. Laughing with him felt good.

"I don't mind confessing to you that I have felt doubt in my life. And I still do today. I hope you don't think me less of a man for it."

"No indeed. I think you a better man for being able to admit it."

He leaned toward her, close enough that she could breathe the pleasant scent of his clean skin. "I must tell you, Mrs. MacGregor looked like an immovable mountain when she first opened the door."

"You are too silly." Her merry chuckle filled the air. "You know, when I was a child, I used to be just a wee bit afraid of her myself. But then I grew taller than her, you see." She clamped her mouth shut. She had forgotten Averil was shorter than she! How many times would she err in her speech today? Such nervousness and missteps weren't like her. She wasn't sure she liked being so tense.

If he found insult in her observation, Averil didn't miss a beat. "Tall or short, you're a mighty fine salesgirl, Miss Cecily. Maybe you and I should be a team."

"I appreciate the flattery, but if I hadn't known Mrs. Mac-Gregor since I was a little girl, she never would have bought a carpet renovator from me. Or anything else, for that matter." Cecily giggled. "She's always been a bit tight with her money."

"In that case, a sale to her is a victory indeed. And if she didn't know your mother, she never would have bought deluxe accessories," Averil added. "She said she remembers the day you were born. Why do I have a feeling she and your mother have been rivals at least that long?"

"At least that long." She gave his forearm the lightest of touches. "I remember they would have pictures taken and then compare to see which one had the most beautiful children."

"You won, of course."

"I wouldn't be so immodest as to say that." Cecily giggled and steered the conversation to firmer terrain. "We must tell Mother about the accessories. I'm sure as soon as she hears that our neighbor bought the deluxe package, she'll buy one too. Maybe she'll even buy five."

❧

Later that day, Averil returned as promised. After Mrs. Eaton's obvious reluctance to have him join them for lunch, he made sure to schedule his appearance well before the normal dinner hour. The sun was setting. Averil drew his wool topcoat more closely around him to ward off the chill. He could only hope that the chill from Cecily's parents wouldn't match the cold outside.

For the first time, he regretted his agreement with Cecily that he would ask her father if he could escort her to the Celebration of Spring. He remembered Mrs. Eaton's rebuff that morning.

*At least I won't be asking her mother if I can be her escort. Praise the Lord for that!*

The instant Averil rang the door chime, Cecily answered. Her eyes sparkled as she invited him in. She tilted her head toward his. The scent of gardenias wafted from her. The enticing aroma had become as familiar as the increasing heartbeat he felt whenever she was near.

"You didn't forget, did you?" she whispered.

Averil realized that Cecily had made her question coy in order to save face in the event he had decided he didn't plan to escort her to the Celebration of Spring, after all. In response, he crafted his answer to be unmistakable. "Forget the Celebration of Spring? Of course not!"

She clasped her right hand to her lace-covered throat as though she were relieved. Averil tried to not laugh aloud. Imagine! How could this lovely creature worry that he had changed his mind?

"There you are, Mr. Kingsley," Mr. Eaton interrupted. "We've been expecting you."

"Good evening. I hope this is a convenient time."

"Most convenient." Mr. Eaton handed him a bank draft. "I trust this is satisfactory."

Averil checked. "Yes. The remainder is due upon delivery of your new machine and one set of deluxe attachments."

"Deluxe? I thought she ordered standard."

"Um, she changed her mind and ordered deluxe. It seems your neighbor—"

Mr. Eaton lifted his hand. "Say no more. The rivalry between those two will be the death of me yet."

Averil chuckled. "Everything you ordered should arrive in no more than two or three weeks, upon which time I shall make haste to deliver it myself."

"My wife and I shall look forward to seeing you then." He smiled and extended his hand. "Good evening."

"But, Sir, there is just one more matter I'd like to discuss with you." Too nervous to stop himself, Averil continued speaking in a quickly flowing stream of words. "I'd like to escort Miss Cecily to the Celebration of Spring, if you will permit."

As soon as the words had left his mouth, Averil gave himself a swift mental kick. If he'd been thinking straight and not been discombobulated by Cecily's presence, he would have asked to speak to her father in his study rather than making his request known, rather awkwardly, in front of her. As it was, if her father chose to spurn him, Cecily would witness his humiliation.

Mr. Eaton turned to his elder daughter. "Were you aware that Mr. Kingsley would be making this request of me, my dear?"

Cecily responded with several rapid nods. "Yes, Father."

"And. . .er. . .no one else has already spoken for you for that day?"

Averil didn't like the tone of Mr. Eaton's voice. He seemed to be conveying a message to Cecily that Averil wasn't supposed to understand. Cecily was lovely enough to have many suitors, but he couldn't imagine she would ask him to speak to her father if she were betrothed to someone else.

"No, Father. No one has spoken for me for that day."

"That is certainly a surprise." Mr. Eaton chuckled. "Well, well, now. I'm sure that Mr. Kingsley here would make a fine escort, but the Celebration of Spring is three weeks away, and his machines will all be delivered in two weeks. You heard him say so yourself."

Averil lifted his forefinger. "Pardon me, but I did say that your machine will be delivered in two weeks. Since I have the rest of the city and the surrounding area to cover, I'll be here for an indefinite period of time. Well past May, in fact."

"I see." Mr. Eaton hesitated.

"Please, Father?" Cecily begged.

"Escorting your daughter would please me very much," Averil added.

Mr. Eaton cut his glance to Cecily. "Well, if it means that much to you. . ."

"Yes." Cecily's voice didn't rise above a whisper. She looked at the floor, as though stricken by a sudden attack of shyness.

"Thank you for the honor, Sir." Averil nodded to Cecily. "Good evening to you both."

He hurried out with as much dignity as he could muster before Mr. Eaton could change his mind. Unease propelled him to the end of the block. He looked back. Mr. Eaton wasn't running behind him, yelling at him to stop, that he had changed his mind and how dare he even think he could ever escort his daughter anywhere.

As soon as he realized his fears were unfounded, the burning fingers of anger tapped him in the gut. How dare Cecily's parents act coldly to him! Why, he was the son of the owner of the Capital Duster Company! His father's only male heir, Averil expected to own the company—and the considerable wealth it had already generated—one day in the distant future. The Eatons' home was grand, but the Kingsley home was grander. Rather than treating him as an undesirable, parents of eligible ladies back home made certain his name appeared on the guest list of every important function. By the time Averil reached the front porch of the boardinghouse, his breaths were arriving in huffs. How dare they!

*How dare they? But they don't know who you are. They think you're a short salesman, a temporary diversion for their daughter at best. And isn't that what you wanted them to think?*

He stopped in midstep. Yes. That was precisely what he wanted them to think. Escaping his identity was one reason he didn't dispute his father's wishes to establish a company branch in Virginia. He was tired of men who slapped him on the back as though they were his best friends, when they really just wanted the prestige of socializing with him or perhaps a well-compensated position in the company. He was weary of wondering if women showed an interest in him for his position rather than his person. Gold diggers, every one of them. Or at least that's what he suspected.

He had come here as a pioneer, to forge a new identity for himself. To prove to himself that he could make friends and attract women—or at least one special woman—without the accoutrements of wealth and position.

Pity, the process wasn't proving as much fun as he first surmised. But his adventure had already opened his eyes. Though the people in his set back home thought themselves broad-minded, they too would have looked with disdain upon the thought of their daughters being escorted anywhere by a door-to-door salesman.

*Maybe I should tell them who I really am. Then the Eatons would be eager for their daughter to share my company.*

No. He had begun the experiment, and he would stay with it until the bitter end. He would rather be alone for the rest of his life than to have Cecily's love and her parents' approval based on his position rather than his person. Averil allowed himself a little grin. He could see that she had already decided.

❧

"You agreed to *what*?" Mother asked.

"I agreed that Mr. Kingsley could escort Cecily to the Celebration of Spring," Father answered.

"This is unconscionable," Mother protested. "Doesn't he know that she already has a suitor? Why, she's practically betrothed to Delmar."

Roger, watching the exchange with youthful curiosity, stopped chewing the rather large sandwich he had slapped together long enough to interrupt. "Delmar? What would Cecily want to be with him for?"

Mother glared at her youngest child. "You may be excused, Roger."

"Aww, I never get to hear anything. If you'll let me stay, I promise to be quiet."

"You heard your mother," Father warned. "You may be excused."

"Yes, Sir." Roger let out an exaggerated sigh. "Who cares about mushy stuff, anyway? I'll go see if Junior's home. Can we go to the ballfield, Father?"

He nodded.

"I want you to be back before dinner," Mother added.

"I will."

Cecily and her parents watched Roger saunter out of the kitchen. As soon as they heard the bang of the back door,

Mother began in earnest. "As I was saying, this carpet renovator salesman is no gentleman in my book. Why, I have a great mind to tell him to cancel my order!"

"There, there, Dear," Father said. "No need to vex yourself."

"I didn't mention Delmar to Mr. Kingsley, so it's my fault, not his, if you think he's not a gentleman," Cecily interjected. "Mother, I hate to disappoint you, but my betrothal to Delmar is a figment of your imagination. Of this whole family's imagination, in fact."

"But he would make a fine match for you," Mother protested.

Cecily crossed her arms over her chest and planted her feet on the floor. "Not if I say he doesn't."

"Why, Cecily!" Mother exclaimed. "How dare you be so disrespectful. Go to your room this instant."

"I am sorry, Mother," Cecily answered.

"That should be enough," Father countered. "Cecily, you may stay here."

"Fine," Mother agreed. "Cecily can hear for herself how ungentlemanly this Mr. Kingsley is for asking a betrothed woman anywhere. No matter what you say, Cecily, I know for a fact that Delmar has eyes for you. His mother and I were speaking about it at the garden club meeting just last Wednesday afternoon."

"Perhaps you and Mrs. Williams should agree to become betrothed to each other," Father quipped.

"This is no joking matter! Our elder daughter's future is at stake." Mother surveyed Cecily. "The Lord endowed you with many fine qualities. A beautiful voice and a fine mind. But He didn't grant you great beauty. You must remember that when selecting from potential suitors. Don't be in such a hurry to discard a fine boy such as Delmar."

Father responded, "Would you be so eager to see this match if Delmar didn't stand well over six feet?"

"Certainly his considerable height is a factor," Mother admitted.

"He is the only boy in Cecily's set who is taller than she." Mother glanced at the ceiling. "Haven't you noticed that the top of Mr. Kingsley's head barely reaches Cecily's earlobe?"

"I'm sure that fact bothers you more than it does me," Cecily countered.

"Truly," Father agreed, "I would rather see our daughter enjoy wedded bliss with someone of diminutive stature than to spend a life of misery with a giant."

"Even if he is poor?" Mother asked.

"Just because he sells carpet renovators doesn't mean he's poor. I'll have you know he's a very good salesman. You've seen so yourself," Cecily pointed out.

"Perhaps he does make a decent wage," Mother admitted. "But that's not the point."

"Then what is the point?" Cecily asked.

Mother didn't answer.

"I think I know," Cecily speculated. "You really don't think Mr. Kingsley is good enough. He wouldn't be good enough if he were seven feet tall."

"No one is good enough for our daughter. Not really." Father's smile was bittersweet.

Cecily sent a grateful smile to her father. At least he understood her.

"I have your best interests at heart too," Mother said.

"I know you do, Mother." Cecily told no lie. Mother had made a good match for herself. Wouldn't any reasonable mother want to see a repeat of such a successful history?

"Whether you admit it to yourself or not," Mother continued, "you have become accustomed to a certain lifestyle, one that requires that your future husband be well situated. Not only does Delmar come from wealth, but his schooling will assure that he will succeed on his own."

"I'm sure it will," Cecily agreed. "But what if Delmar isn't the one for me? What if the Lord wants me to learn the art of sacrifice?"

"As with many things the Lord wants from us, the art of sacrifice is more easily opined upon than practiced," Mother observed. "Lest you think your father and I are concerned merely about money, think again. What about this salesman's character? What do you really know about him, Cecily? We've only seen him a few times."

"I know that he's witty, and attractive, and charming. And most important, he loves the Lord."

"I am in no position to argue that. I know you're trusting, and that's not entirely undesirable." Mother's voice grew soft. "But what if Mr. Kingsley is merely using you? Mrs. MacGregor told me all that transpired when she bought her Capital Duster. Why, you sold the carpet renovator for him! I'm sure he knows you have many friends and acquaintances. Did it ever occur to you that he may want to meet your friends in hopes of gaining their confidence to increase his sales?"

"Of course not! How can you say that?" Cecily felt herself shaking with anger. "Mother, please excuse me."

"Certainly. I want you to think about what I said."

Cecily made haste to reach her room, then shut the door behind her with a gentle but firm thud. She was growing fond of Averil. She didn't know how her feelings could have developed so quickly, but they had. So why did Mother have to introduce doubts in her mind? No, Averil couldn't be using her. He just couldn't.

*But what if Mother were right?*

## seven

Cecily heard a knock on the door of her room. She was in no mood to see anyone, even if the visitor was Mother hoping to make amends. Perhaps if she didn't respond, whoever it was would give up and go away. Arms folded, Cecily continued to stare past the white lace curtains that decorated her window. Her gaze set upon the centuries-old oak tree that had been a familiar part of the view from her room ever since she could remember. She could see Mrs. MacGregor's no-nonsense brick Georgian home. What a contrast to the many-gabled brick Victorian the Eatons called home!

Urgent knocks interrupted her musings.

"Yes?" she answered, reluctance evident in her voice.

"It's me," Augusta said. "Open up."

Augusta. Cecily wasn't in the humor to see her sister, either. But perhaps another opinion would do her good. Cecily opened the door.

Augusta entered and then shut the door behind her. "I heard you talking with Mother and Father. What was all the commotion about?"

"They don't want me to think about Averil as a potential suitor. Especially Mother. She doesn't think he's good enough." Cecily sighed as she plopped herself on the bed she had slept in since she was a child. "I know Mother has her standards, but I never thought she'd actually say something like that and mean it."

Augusta sat beside her. "Oh, that." She blew out a breath that showed her exasperation. "You know how emotional Mother gets, especially when it comes to us and our suitors. Not that I have any suitors." Augusta clasped her hands and looked toward the sky as if in a dreamlike trance. "I know I have to wait for you to get married before I can, since you're older than me. But you're so lucky, Cecily. You have two suitors, and I don't have any."

"Averil isn't a suitor, at least not yet. He's just escorting me to the Celebration of Spring."

"If he's thinking of courting you, he can't go much more public than that," Augusta countered. "You know all of our friends will be there."

Cecily swallowed. Augusta was right! Her sister's point made her realize that she didn't mind the prospect of appearing in the open with Averil.

"Just you wait," Augusta continued. "He'll be a suitor soon enough. He likes you. He likes you a lot."

Cecily's heart beat faster at the thought. "How can you tell?"

Augusta's dreamy look returned. "I can see it in his eyes."

"I don't know." Cecily cast her gaze to the beige-and-green rug. If her misjudgment of Professor Tobias proved any indication, Augusta didn't have the faintest notion of who harbored romantic inclinations toward whom. Still, the thought that Averil's interest was obvious to others was a pleasant one indeed.

"No matter what you say, you're the lucky one." Augusta sighed. "I do miss Professor Tobias ever so much. I almost wish you still took lessons with him. Then at least he'd come by the house."

Remembering her colossal error during her solo in church, Cecily thought that to answer would be folly. Uncomfortable, she stood up and paced the room.

Augusta rose and threw her arms around Cecily. "I'm so glad you stopped, though. The thought of him passing me by while going in the music room alone with you to give you a lesson—well, not that there would ever be anything the least bit improper taking place. Still. . ." Augusta squeezed Cecily's waist. "I'm so glad I don't have to witness that."

Cecily tightened her grip on Augusta and then let go. "Anything for you."

Augusta nodded as she sent Cecily a grateful, crooked grin, the same one she always used whenever Cecily did her a favor. The first time Cecily remembered seeing that grin was when she had shared her ice cream with the then six-year-old Augusta. Cecily couldn't resist sending her own crooked grin back.

"So," Augusta prodded, "which one do you like best?"

"Which one what?"

"Which man do you like best, Silly. Delmar or Mr. Kingsley?"

"Oh," was all Cecily could utter. She wasn't sure how else to respond. Her feelings for Averil had snuck up on her without warning. She had never felt for a man what she felt for Averil, yet she knew little about him aside from the fact that he was charming, handsome, and a purveyor of carpet renovators. And she hesitated to share her passions with her romantic, idealistic sister.

"You don't have to tell me." Augusta seated herself back on the bed, folded her arms, and nodded once with confidence. "You like Mr. Kingsley much better. I don't blame you, even if you are a head taller than he is."

"That doesn't bother me," Cecily was quick to point out. Did the fact that she towered over him bother Averil? She hoped not.

"As long as it doesn't bother the two of you, why should anyone else care?" Augusta said. "Besides, who'd want to be with Delmar? He's such a bore." She wrinkled her nose.

"You and our brother seem to share that opinion."

"And Father too, if I read him correctly," Augusta said. "Pity he couldn't be more exciting."

Cecily laughed. "You'll have to fight off your share of bores soon enough."

"If Professor Tobias doesn't speak up soon, I'm not sure I'd even resist a bore." Augusta giggled. "The idea of men coming to fisticuffs over me does sound thrilling, but I'll have to wait. I'll just have to watch them scuffle over you at the celebration."

"Scuffle? Over me?" Cecily scoffed. "Don't be silly. I can't imagine two mature and reasonable men coming to blows over any girl."

"They just might, once the bidding starts over the boxed lunches," Augusta persisted.

Cecily groaned. "That's right. The bachelor bids."

"Yes!" Augusta's voice rose in pitch equivalent to her excitement. "I'll bet Delmar and Mr. Kingsley come to blows over yours."

Cecily shook her head. "That won't be necessary."

"No. They can just empty out their pockets." Augusta's mouth twisted. "At least the money will go to a good cause."

At that moment, Mother called to Augusta from the kitchen.

"I forgot," Augusta said. "It's my turn to set the table and dry the dishes. I wish we could afford a live-in maid instead of letting Hattie go home every night."

"I suspect that even if Hattie lived with us, Mother would still want us to know the meaning of work."

"I suppose," Augusta agreed, letting out a dramatic sigh before leaving the room.

Cecily's uplifted mood lasted only a short time before she turned contemplative. What would happen at the Celebration of Spring? She didn't want Averil to try to outbid Delmar on her basket. Despite what she had told her mother about his making good money on commissions, Cecily doubted he could afford to spend extra money on a luxury. Delmar's pockets, on the other hand, were deep. He could outbid almost anyone in the city, should he set his mind to do so. If the bidding got hot, Cecily knew who would win. And who would lose. The thought of the projected outcome didn't please her.

"What's wrong with you, Cecily?" she asked herself. "What has made you so vain today? What gives you the right to think even one man would bid on your basket, let alone two? Even worse, what makes you think you should control the outcome? Isn't everything in God's hands?"

She thought about the events of the day and her mother's

opposition to Averil. She knew her mother spoke out of love. She wanted what was best for her daughter. Wouldn't any mother?

The nagging doubt that Mother could be right was even worse than her unfettered opposition. What if Averil was just using her? After all, he did show up at their church without notice. But then again, he had said their house of worship was the only one within walking distance of the boardinghouse. Cecily tried to remember the nearby churches. If memory served her well, Averil was right. There was no other church within walking distance for him. At least not easy walking distance. She remembered his keen answers during Sunday school and the knowledge of the Bible he displayed. Surely someone who seemed to be as strong a Christian as Averil wouldn't use the Lord's house and His Word as instruments to further himself socially or in business.

No. Mother was wrong about that. She had to be.

But what about Delmar? Cecily shook her head with enough force to dislodge the picture of the would-be suitor from her mind's eye. Augusta was right. Delmar was a bore. All he ever talked about was prestige, power, and how he planned to become a huge success in life's endeavors. Cecily supposed in this day and age a man was expected to harbor some ambitions, but Delmar seemed not to make a move unless it would further his future, somehow. She knew what he wanted: the right schooling, the right street addresses for his residence as well as his office, and, of course, the right wife. Was she the one? Her family seemed to think so.

*Lord, what will Thou have me do? I don't want to disobey Mother, but I don't feel Delmar is the man I want to spend the rest of my life with.*

Cecily sat on her vanity chair in stillness. She studied her reflection in the mirror, but the image reflected back at her barely registered. The state of the soul was the Lord's prominent concern. She had always tried to keep her soul safe from sin and its subsequent consequences. For how else could she continue to commune with God? She had known all her life that God had a plan for her. He would reveal it in His own time. If He wanted her to be with someone other than Averil, He would let her know. No man would put a stop to God's plan. She would just have to wait and see what He revealed, that's all.

Or was she pushing the issue of whom she would eventually marry, prodding God to give her an answer now because she felt she was ready? Cecily had never been wildly popular with potential suitors, but she wasn't a wallflower, either. So why was it that no other man had made her brain seem to disengage itself from coherent thought whenever he was near? Whenever she saw Averil, it seemed as though her mouth started moving on its own.

*Why is that? Perhaps you haven't been listening to Me.*

The voice resounded as clearly as though the Lord Himself were sitting beside her. Perhaps her mouth seemed to move on its own because of her excitement over meeting Averil. He was a new man who exuded such confidence, such life, such possibilities! Had she rushed to encourage him without giving this new association enough thought? Had she not taken enough time to speak with the Lord about Averil and what, if any, role he should play in her life?

"Lord," she prayed, "please be with me in all my relationships. Guide me in my dealings with my parents. Let me not disrespect or dishonor them in any way, Lord, for I know that to do so would be the same as dishonoring Thee. Help me be a good sister to Augusta and a good sister and an example of womanhood to Roger. I also ask that Thou wilt be with me as I conduct my friendship with Averil. I pray that his motives are pure and that I won't be disappointed. But if I am, help me to learn from my mistake. In the precious name of Jesus Christ my Savior. Amen."

As soon as Cecily finished uttering her prayer, she realized that Averil would be the one to grapple with his conscience if he were only using her. As long as her own conduct remained above reproach, she had nothing to fear.

*And if Mother is right and I'm meant to be with Delmar, nothing will stop His plan.*

She could only pray that the Lord had other ideas.

❧

"You will be joining us for dinner, won't you, Mr. Kingsley?" Cecily asked him after class the next Sunday. She held her breath. Thanks to her gentle prodding, he had already sat beside them in their family pew once again. Cecily sent him a shy smile. She had prayed for patience all week, but her actions defied her request. *There goes my mouth again.*

As she chastised herself, she knew in her heart she wasn't sorry.

Averil broke out into one of his most charming smiles. "I'd be delighted." His face darkened almost as quickly. "Um, your parents won't mind, will they?"

"Oh, no. They'll be pleased to have you dine with us." Cecily knew for her sake they would pretend to be pleased whether they really were or not. She decided to press on, lest he express further doubt. "Cook goes out of her way on Sundays. She always bakes a fabulous roast of beef with gravy and the creamiest mashed potatoes you ever put in your mouth It's not to be missed."

"Sounds like a mouthwatering treat."

Roger came up behind them. "Hey, Sis. Mother says it's time to go."

"Certainly." Cecily knew the word sounded terse with disappointment. She wished to prolong her time in semiprivacy with Averil.

Roger eyed Averil as he kept in step with them. "He's coming along too?"

"Yes," Cecily said. "He's invited to dinner."

Roger shrugged with the indifference of his youth.

Quick-witted as always, Averil didn't let questions linger.

Instead, he launched into a conversation about the latest enthusiasm, physical fitness. Roger grinned from ear to ear and obliged without missing a beat. Roger had recently started going to the gymnasium after school to lift weights with his friends. Only an instant passed before Roger was flexing his still-scrawny biceps for Averil to admire.

Cecily wondered how Averil managed to hit upon Roger's favorite subject. Having never spent time in gymnasiums herself, she was content to walk beside them and lose herself in the sights and sounds of spring while their voices droned in the background.

She sighed as she drank in the beauty of a Virginia spring. Plentiful dogwood trees blossomed. Some were pink, but most were white. Azaleas were in full bloom, adding pink, red, and white blooms to the landscape. The flowers' brilliance was striking alongside a carpet of new green grass. An occasional squirrel chattered and played, unafraid of people walking nearby. She wished she had a few nuts to feed them, as she often did in winter.

All too soon, they caught up to Cecily's parents and sister.

"Mr. Kingsley," Mother said, the question in her voice obvious.

"I invited him to eat dinner with us," Cecily hurried to explain.

"Indeed? What a fine idea," Father said.

"Mr. Kingsley knows all about athletics," Roger added. "He goes to a gymnasium in New York. He's even promised to show me a few moves on the basketball court sometime."

"Why, that's fine," Father agreed. "I didn't know you were interested in athletics, Mr. Kingsley."

"I'm afraid my interest far exceeds my skill," Averil answered.

"Now, I'll bet you're just being modest," Father protested.

Cecily didn't mind that the male members of their party obsessed about their own topic. She was just glad Averil was part of their band, walking beside her as though he belonged right there.

As the men talked and Mother pretended to listen, Augusta

tugged on Cecily's sleeve. "What do you think Mother would say if I invited Norman to dinner next week?" she whispered.

"The new boy? The one with dark hair?"

"That's the one."

Cecily shook her head. "I can't believe you've developed a new crush already."

"Not really." Augusta shrugged. "I just think he's handsome, that's all."

Mother interrupted. "What are you two girls whispering about?"

"Nothing," they answered in unison.

Mother cut her glance to them, a sure sign she doubted the truth behind their words.

"I recommend that you proceed slowly," Cecily whispered as they reached the edge of their front lawn. "I'm having enough trouble as it is."

&

Cecily was sorry to see the end of dinner arrive. Before she realized what had happened, the meal had flown by, with lively conversation filling the air in nonstop pleasantness. The clock gonged to announce two hours past noon as they made their way to the foyer.

"Well, it was mighty pleasurable to have you join us for dinner, Mr. Kingsley," Father observed.

"And a delicious meal it was. Everything that Miss Eaton promised and more. The creamed potatoes were just as you promised. Truly the best I've ever tasted. Not to mention the exquisite coconut cake. She hadn't even told me how delectable it would be!"

"I had to save something for a surprise," Cecily joked.

"You succeeded. And the company was even finer." Averil shot a meaningful look at Cecily and then directly at Mother.

"And to think, only a short time ago, you were just another door-to-door salesman, asking us to buy a carpet renovator,"

Mother noted. "How fortunate for us that you will be staying in the city. I do believe you alluded to the possibility during the meal?"

"He did," Father agreed. "I'm afraid we digressed before he could fill us in completely."

"That is quite all right. I am the one who is fortunate to be staying in the city," Averil answered. "I must admit, I was skating on thin ice when I first arrived here. I was sent here to test the waters, to see how our carpet renovator would sell in this region. I'm pleased to report that sales have been brisk. So brisk, in fact, that I just received word yesterday that the plans are moving full-steam ahead. I'll be setting up a new office. Richmond will be company headquarters for the Mid-Atlantic Region."

Cecily gasped. Her hand flew to her open mouth. "Really? Mr. Kingsley, that's wonderful!"

"Wonderful, indeed." Averil looked into Cecily's eyes. "I have you to thank, at least in part."

"Not really." She sent her gaze to the Oriental rug that had once nearly been the demise of the Capital Duster's success.

"Of course I must thank you. First, you, Mrs. Eaton," he said, turning his attention to Mother, "for buying a machine from me."

"That is quite all right. I'm sure I'll be quite pleased with my renovator."

"I hope so." A sheepish look crossed his countenance. "I'm afraid I have some bad news. Because of the increase in sales, the delivery of your renovator will be delayed."

"Not too long, I hope."

"Only by a week or so. I hope this won't inconvenience you too much."

"I suppose not," Mrs. Eaton said, though doubt clouded her voice.

"That really is good news for your company, though," Cecily observed. "Isn't it? I mean, for sales to be so vigorous."

He nodded. "Indeed. I must thank you, Miss Eaton, for helping me get off to an auspicious start here. I suppose I can tell you now, I was a bit worried Mrs. MacGregor would complain to her friends and spoil my chances of selling another machine within a hundred miles of here. But you straightened all of that out. And now that I've sold so many carpet renovators since my arrival, the company thinks the move to establish a regional office here is justified."

"So you'll be staying indefinitely." Cecily knew her voice betrayed her excitement. She cast her gaze to the bouquet of spring flowers on the hall table and made a show of adjusting an errant bloom in hopes of mitigating the delight she knew she must be emanating.

"Yes," he confirmed.

Cecily looked into his handsome face, doing her best not to smile too widely. Averil's sparkling eyes indicated the prospect was not displeasing to him—or at least she hoped so.

"I trust your move means a hefty promotion for you?" Father inquired.

"Um, you could say that." He nodded.

"My most hearty congratulations, my boy." Father slapped him on the back. "Well, now, I'm sure we'll be seeing you again soon. That would be a fine thing."

"Fine, indeed," Averil agreed.

Cecily wasn't ready to bid him a good afternoon. "The outdoors seems inviting. I do believe I would like to sit on the porch swing for a few moments."

Mother raised an eyebrow. "Only for a few moments."

Relieved to have gained permission, Cecily followed Averil onto the porch. "The spring air is so pleasant. I just had to get out of the house."

"Yes, spring is a lovely time of year. I look forward to a brisk promenade home." He paused.

Cecily's heart beat faster with a sudden feeling of nervousness. "I'm so glad you'll be escorting me to the Celebration of Spring," she managed to utter.

"As am I." He waited.

Cecily was grateful that he apparently could see she had something to say. She took in a breath. "I need to tell you a secret," she said in a low voice in case Mother was eavesdropping. "Promise you won't tell?"

"I would never betray a lady's confidence." He kept his voice just above a whisper.

She darted her eyes back and forth before speaking. After deciding that no one was within hearing range, she said, "My box. It will be green with three lilies on top."

"Your box?"

"You don't know?" This was going to be harder than she expected. Was she in the process of making a fool of herself?

"Know what?"

She studied his face to see if he were toying with her. His oblique look told her he had no inkling what she meant. "My box lunch. All the unmarried ladies make them, and the bachelors bid on them." Feeling herself blush, she examined the small ruby stone on her right ring finger as though she had never seen it before. She dug her heel into the floor of the verandah.

"That sounds like a charming custom," he proclaimed in a gentle tone.

She kept her gaze on the ruby. "I–I suppose I'm being too bold to say anything. You don't have to bid on it if you don't want to."

"Why, I wouldn't think of bidding on anyone else's."

Cecily looked into his ebony eyes, eyes that reminded her of obsidian, only not so cold and hard. His promise left her feeling more excited about the Celebration of Spring. As waves of joy washed over her, Cecily realized she felt more anticipation about the celebration than she had felt about anything else in a long time.

# eight

Averil could hardly contain his excitement as he drove his new buggy past the gate of the boys' school, with the most beautiful young woman he had ever known sitting by his side. He had looked forward to the celebration as soon as Cecily's parents had agreed to allow him to be her escort, but the reality of being so near to Cecily on such a festive day didn't register with him until she was sitting beside him in the open-air buggy. He wished he could detour all through the city—and not to show everyone the company name imprinted on both sides of his buggy. He wished he could show everyone who was anyone that the prettiest girl in the state of Virginia was riding with him—Averil Kingsley—to the Celebration of Spring.

He managed to contain himself, but made sure to sneak a sideways peek at the vision perched beside him. "My, but I do believe this lovely day pales in comparison to your beauty, Miss Eaton," he ventured. "If I may be so bold."

She let out a delightfully melodic giggle, then smoothed her skirt even though the fabric wasn't wrinkled in the least. "Mr. Kingsley, how you do talk!"

Making sure not to keep his eyes off the road for too many moments at a time, Averil studied her with his peripheral vision. Dressed in pure white in anticipation of the Maypole dance, Cecily wore a hat with an exceedingly large brim that framed her face to perfection. The hat boasted an abundance of silk roses. Averil wondered why Cecily's head didn't tip forward from the weight, but contrary to the laws of gravity, she kept her head upright and her gaze level. She carried a matching white parasol as extra insurance to protect her creamy complexion from the sun's harsh rays.

Riding along in the buggy, he realized he was much less conscious than usual of the fact that she towered over him. With the fashions of styling their hair in billowing chignons, wearing large hats, and holding parasols, only the tallest man accompanying the most diminutive woman could hope to sit higher than his female companion. Nevertheless, he remembered the numerous occasions where Cecily shared conversations with him while they both stood, forcing her to look downward into his face. She never seemed to notice and certainly was never vexed. For her consideration, he was grateful.

"A penny for your thoughts, Mr. Kingsley."

He didn't mind his pensive mood being interrupted by such a sweet voice. "I doubt my thoughts are worth that much."

"I'm sure mine aren't."

"I'll venture a guess that any thought that runs through your pretty head is worth at least that much. Maybe even double." He paused, waiting for her to respond.

Instead, she looked around the school play yard. Catching the gaze of another woman who seemed to be about her age, Cecily waved a gloved hand. The woman smiled and waved in return. Averil wondered if the friend noticed that Cecily was riding with someone new. If she did, the woman showed no signs of curiosity. Averil couldn't help but feel a twinge of disappointment that no one seemed to think it out of the ordinary that he was escorting Cecily.

"I was just thinking how much I agree with you that this is a perfectly fine day, Mr. Kingsley," she finally said. She looked up at the blue sky. "A perfectly fine day indeed."

The festivities had been due to begin fifteen minutes before they arrived. Judging from the frivolous mood enveloping the campus, the party was in full swing. Cecily was expected to line up for the Maypole dance just before lunch, and Averil had no desire to bear the responsibility for any tardiness on Cecily's part. He heaved a sigh of relief when he spotted one last hitching post vacant. He drew the carriage up to it, and after he helped Cecily disembark, Averil tapped his foot in rhythm with the lively band music as he hitched his horse.

"I do so like this tune." Cecily swayed back and forth, ever so slightly, in time to the rhythm.

"Yet another thing on which you and I are in hearty agreement."

Knowing Cecily wouldn't mind, he paused for a moment to stroke General on the side of the neck. General's nondescript brown coat and gray eyes caused him to fade into the background among brilliant white steeds or black Arabian mares, but General was gentle and willing to take Averil—and his guest—wherever he wanted to go. That's all he asked. Averil took a moment to move his hand from the horse's scruffy neck to the long hairs of his dark brown mane. The hair felt smooth and tangle-free since the stable boy had just brushed him that morning. Averil pulled an apple out of his pocket and fed it to the faithful animal. General snorted his gratitude. Now that Averil's business was scheduled to expand, he'd be relying on General more than ever.

At that moment, he realized he had perhaps kept Cecily waiting too long. "I beg your pardon for keeping you. I know General will be standing here awhile. I hate to leave him, poor thing, after he has pulled us along here by himself. I will be purchasing a companion for him within a few days." Averil patted General on the neck once more.

"I'm sure he'll welcome the help." Her features were relaxed, indicating she wasn't the least bit perturbed. "I like a man who is considerate of his horse. It usually means he is kind to people too."

"I find that if I display courtesy to others, be they animal or human, life is a much more pleasant affair for all concerned."

"I couldn't agree more."

As they made their way through the thick of the festivities, he patted his chest to ascertain that his money remained inside the inner pocket of his blue-and-white-striped seersucker suit. Wanting to make sure he had enough cash to make a successful bid on Cecily's boxed lunch, that morning he had tucked a few extra dollars in his money clip.

A bespectacled man with an anemic look tipped his hat. "Good morning, Miss Eaton."

"Good morning, Professor Tobias." Cecily looked at Averil. "Have you met my former music instructor?"

"I don't believe I've had the pleasure." Averil touched the brim of his straw hat. He wondered why Professor Tobias no longer instructed her in music. Was he the same teacher Augusta had been singing with the day he first knocked on their door? Or had they progressed to a new teacher? He made a mental note to ask sometime when they weren't surrounded by a crowd.

After Cecily introduced Averil to Professor Tobias, the teacher said, "I greatly regret that you must use the word 'former' to describe me, Miss Eaton. I do wish I were still your music teacher."

"How nice of you to say that, but I'm quite confident that my slot has long been taken by some other lucky student." Cecily turned to Averil. "Professor Tobias is an accomplished musician. He is quite in demand, you know."

"I'll remember that should someone ask me to recommend a good teacher." Lest he should be recruited as a new student on the spot, Averil hastened to add, "I tried my hand at piano as a boy, to disastrous results, I'm afraid."

"I'm sure you exaggerate." Even as she spoke, Cecily surveyed the crowd. Her eyes lit up and she started to move away. "I see someone else I want you to meet, Mr. Kingsley. If you'll pardon us, Professor Tobias?"

"But of course." The music teacher's voice held no enthusiasm.

Averil allowed himself to be introduced to a number of Cecily's friends. He greeted them all politely and exchanged pleasantries. All the while, his stomach tied itself in a knot. This outing was the first where he and Cecily appeared together, with the exception of church services and Sunday school class. He had a feeling he would be meeting many of her friends and acquaintances. What would they think? He had been so concerned about making a favorable impression on Cecily and her parents that he hadn't stopped to think he would have to extend his efforts even further.

Why did meeting Cecily's friends and acquaintances make him so anxious? Being nervous wasn't like him. He was a door-to-door salesman. He was accustomed to greeting people every day, strangers he didn't know. But then, he had something to say—a great deal to say—about the stupendous Capital Duster Electric Pneumatic Carpet Renovator.

Without his machine, what would he talk about?

*Please, Lord, be with me now.*

Apparently the Lord was listening, because Averil didn't make any noticeable gaffs during any of the introductions. Her friends pretended not to notice how much shorter he stood than Cecily. Before he knew it, the time for the Maypole dance had arrived. Averil breathed an audible sigh of relief. Finally he could just enjoy watching the event and listening to the music.

Once a lilting tune started, ladies, all dressed in white, skipped around the pole in time to the beat, each holding a ribbon. Averil looked for Cecily among the group. Spotting her among the others was easy, since she was more than a head taller than all but two or three of the other ladies. Her lithe form moved with grace and elegance as she met each dancer and either lifted her pale blue ribbon or ducked so that the fabric she held wove over or under as appropriate. Round and round they went. The ribbons, which had blown freely in the breeze, were woven around the pole until only a foot of each piece remained unfettered. The white pole was now decorated with a myriad of pastel colors that reminded Averil of Easter eggs. He was among the most animated of the enthusiastic audience who gasped, whooped, and applauded to show their appreciation. The five-piece band, situated under a wooden gazebo decorated in festive ribbon for the occasion, broke out into yet another spirited tune. A grand celebration of spring had begun in earnest.

"Look," said Cecily. "Everyone's gathering near the stage."

"Will we be treated to a play as well?"

Cecily shook her head, then tilted her face toward a man who had taken his place near the center. "That's Hank, the auctioneer. He's ready to start the bidding on the boxed lunches."

"Come." She took his hand to lead him. He could feel the pleasant warmth of her fingers, even through the cotton gloves she wore. As soon as she reached what she thought was a good spot, only a few feet from the auctioneer, she let go of his hand.

She leaned toward him and whispered, "Remember. It's the green box with three lilies."

He pointed to his head. "I've had those details etched in my brain ever since the first time you told me."

She hurried toward the seats on the stage where the single women were meant to sit, but not before casting a pleased look his way.

Averil stood and watched the meals being auctioned, one after the other. He could see from the decorations that the ladies had made every effort to beautify their boxes. Attractive ribbons graced all of them. Flowers were a popular choice for additional decorations. Each one looked as distinctive as the creators themselves. He knew this because after each winner was announced, the lady in question would rise from her seat on the temporary stage and, usually amid giggles, meet the winner. The proud bachelor would then claim his lunch, take the girl by the elbow, and lead her to a vacant spot on the grass, where they could enjoy lunch together in peace. Or at least as much peace as a couple could enjoy during the lively celebration.

Cecily sat at her place in the back, casting glances his way from time to time. As each box came and went, Averil realized he couldn't have identified Cecily's box without her telling him which one was hers.

Finally, the auctioneer chose from the table the box that Averil had been waiting to see. "Now, here's a beauty," Hank declared as he examined Cecily's artwork. He tilted the top toward the crowd so they could get a better look. "Would y'all just take a look at these gorgeous spring flowers on top?" He examined the lilies. "One. Two. Three." He nodded. "Three lovely, giant lilies. Now, I'd bet my bottom dollar that the girl who made this box is as pretty as a fresh spring bouquet herself."

Someone near the back let out a whoop. Averil cut his stare in the direction of the holler in hopes of seeing the man who dared express his approval of Cecily's box in such a vulgar way. Unfortunately he was unable to spot the offender among the poker-faced men.

"Just look at this color!" Hank said. "See how the deep green contrasts with the white flowers."

Averil turned his attention back to the stage. He didn't want to lose the bid out of jealousy.

"I think this is just about the prettiest color green I've ever seen," Hank observed.

Averil eyed Cecily sitting on the stage. Apparently feeling his gaze upon her, she set her glance on him shyly. Her slight smile told him he hadn't made a mistake in identifying the boxed lunch. Not until that instant did the full impact of his promise to bid on it register with him. He would have to raise his hand in front of a sea of people. Averil felt his heart racing.

"Now, who'll give me a dollar for this lovely boxed lunch? Like I said, I'm sure the girl who made it is just as pretty." The auctioneer's compliments and speculations mirrored his comments about all the other entries.

Averil shot his hand into the sky, confident he would be announced the winner.

The auctioneer beamed. "I have three bids for a dollar. Who'll give me one dollar and fifty cents?"

Three bids! Averil looked around.

The auctioneer intoned, "A dollar and a half from the gentleman in beige."

Averil peered in the direction of the auctioneer's stare and spotted Professor Tobias. The music teacher?

"Two dollars?" After the briefest of pauses, the auctioneer said, "Two dollars from the gentleman with the Panama hat."

Averil cut his gaze to find a Panama hat. His errand proved an easy one, since the man wearing the only one in the crowd towered above everyone else. Who in the world could he possibly be? He hoped the man was a friend setting out to make the bidding more interesting or to gain more money for charity.

"Three dollars. Do I hear three dollars? The school sure could use the money," the auctioneer cajoled.

Averil watched, astonished to observe the tall man and the music teacher try to outbid each other. Soon, Cecily's lunch was going for ten dollars, almost as much as Averil had brought.

A triumphant grin displayed itself on the tall stranger's face. The victorious expression made his features look handsome—almost. Averil wondered who the stranger could possibly be. Cecily had never mentioned a suitor, and he couldn't imagine a mere friend being willing to take bidding on a boxed lunch up so high, even to benefit the school.

He saw from his peripheral vision that Cecily shifted in her seat. She set her brown eyes toward his face, but he averted his gaze. He wouldn't disappoint her. Not if he could help it.

"Eleven dollars!" the teacher bid.

Averil waited for the tall man to bid. He fumbled in his pockets, but apparently came up empty. His face reddening, he grumbled under his breath. Finally he shrugged his shoulders and shook his head.

The auctioneer nodded. "Eleven dollars, going once—"

Averil shouted, "Eleven fifty!"

The auctioneer smiled and looked at Averil. "Wonderful! Our first bidder is back! You're a smart man, my friend in the blue seersucker suit."

Several people nearby turned to see the first bidder. Some sent him approving nods. Others were slack jawed. Still others furrowed their brows in apparent curiosity.

"Eleven seventy-five," Professor Tobias persisted.

Averil gulped. He had twelve dollars in his vest. Reaching into his pocket, he could feel a dime and three pennies. "Twelve dollars and thirteen cents!"

"We have a bid for twelve dollars and thirteen cents," the auctioneer informed the crowd.

Snickering and whispering ensued. Averil tightened his jaw. The embarrassment was worth everything, as long as he had outbid the teacher.

"Twelve dollars and thirteen cents going once." The auctioneer paused and surveyed the crowd. "Twelve dollars and thirteen cents going twice."

"Fifteen dollars!" Professor Tobias cried.

The crowd, including Averil, let out a collective gasp. Fifteen dollars! Hushed comments rippled through the throng.

"Fifteen dollars going once," Hank shouted.

As much as he wanted to bid sixteen dollars, Averil couldn't. For a split second, he even considered borrowing the difference from someone. But who? Certainly not Mr. Eaton. Averil didn't know anybody else.

"Fifteen dollars going twice." The auctioneer paused.

No, he couldn't prolong the bidding. He would just have to let Cecily lunch with the music teacher. Though disappointed, he stood to his full height to mask his displeasure with this turn of events. He had a rival in his affection for Cecily!

"Sold for fifteen dollars!"

## nine

As bidding began on the next box, Cecily and her lunch companion made their way through the throng. Averil studied Cecily's expression. Her mouth was open as though she felt distressed, but anger didn't color her face. As the couple snaked their way through the crowd, he noticed they drew closer to where he stood. Averil became conscious of his beating heart but tried to keep a nonchalant expression on his face. Finally Cecily paused in front of him.

"Will you do me a favor? I want you to bid on Augusta's basket," she whispered.

Her suggestion startled Averil. The thought hadn't occurred to him. "Really?"

"Yes. Please do." She lowered her voice so he could barely hear her.

"But—"

"Then the four of us can sit together," she hissed.

Aha! So she wanted to sit with him after all. "Which box?"

"The blue one with the gingham ribbon."

"All right," he answered. "I'll do my best to win this time."

Professor Tobias tugged on Cecily's sleeve. "We'd best be moving along unless we want all the good spots to be taken."

"Yes," she agreed in a voice that sounded more loud and cheerful than necessary. She turned back to Averil. "We'll try to sit in the pine grove."

"The pine grove?"

"Yes." She tilted her head toward a cluster of tall trees near the edge of the grounds.

The music teacher cut his glance to Averil. The hard glint in his eyes was apparent even behind thick spectacles. Just as quickly, he changed his expression to one more pleasant and addressed Cecily. "I know you are doing your best to be polite. After all, Mr. Kingsley is a stranger in the city, and admittedly he made a substantial bid on your box. But perhaps, Miss Eaton, he may wish to bid on another box and enjoy lunch with one of the other lovely young ladies."

"Yes, indeed," Cecily responded without a bit of rancor. "In fact, I was just suggesting to Mr. Kingsley that he might bid on Augusta's box."

"What a kind gesture. But should he win, I'm sure he and Miss Augusta can find a place to sit on their own." He took Cecily's elbow, a gesture that made Averil want to swat his hand off her like a fly. "Come along."

Cecily obeyed but not before sending Averil a doe-eyed look.

Averil ignored Professor Tobias and looked toward the auctioneer. He had disappointed Cecily once. He wasn't about to be stymied again.

Augusta remained on stage with a rather plain woman who couldn't stop giggling. Averil knew he needed to pay attention. He had to win this bid!

Hank, the auctioneer, chose a blue box wrapped with a gingham bow. Since the last box remaining on the table was pink, the one in Hank's hands had to be Augusta's. Averil paid rapt attention.

"Now," the auctioneer said, "as y'all can plainly see, one of these pretty ladies has put a great deal of effort into preparing this outstanding boxed lunch. I know just by looking at this gorgeous box that whoever wins this bid will be a lucky bachelor indeed! Whose favorite color is blue? Let me see a show of hands."

Several hands shot up amid scattered applause.

"In that case, the bidding on this box should be an event to witness. We've had many excellent bids today." He swept his hand toward the last box. "We're getting near the end here, and I know all of you bachelors are hungry. Let's dig down deep and go out with a bang. Who will give me a dollar?"

"One dollar!" Averil raised his hand.

"I have one dollar." The auctioneer looked pleased. "Who'll give me a dollar and a half for this beautiful boxed lunch?"

"A dollar fifty!" a male voice on the opposite end of the group responded.

Averil groaned inaudibly and surveyed the crowd. Who was bidding against him this time? He found the hand lifted in the air. Attached to it was a man still young enough to be called "cute." Averil was certain he recognized him from church.

"One fifty! Do I hear two dollars?"

Averil raised his hand. "Two dollars!"

"Two dollars from the persistent bachelor in the blue seersucker suit," the auctioneer noted.

Much to Averil's chagrin, chuckles rippled through the crowd.

"Two twenty-five!" the young man called out.

Guilt filled Averil's soul. He had no interest in Augusta beyond the fact that she was Cecily's sister, and the young man bidding against him looked much more suited in age to the sweet young woman. But he had promised Cecily he would try to win Augusta's box.

*Lord, I pray I'm doing the right thing.*

"Three dollars!"

"I have three dollars." The auctioneer held up three fingers, then four.

"Do I hear four?"

Silence.

"Three dollars," the auctioneer called out. "Three dollars going once, going twice. Sold to the bachelor in the seersucker suit."

Lukewarm clapping greeted Averil and Augusta as he escorted her from the stand. Averil waved his straw hat to the crowd's applause. Augusta had a broad smile fixed on her face, but Averil could tell from the way her arm tensed that her happiness was all for show. So as not to embarrass her, he made sure his smile was just as wide.

Bidding on the last box diverted the audience's attention away from them not an instant too soon.

Averil tilted his head toward the young woman now sitting alone on the stage. "I suppose everyone knows whose box he's bidding on now, with one lady remaining, eh?" Averil observed to Augusta.

Augusta looked back at the young woman as though she hadn't just been sitting beside her. "That's Lily James. She's been engaged to her beau for years." Augusta shrugged. "Everyone knows he'll bid against her father and brother until the price goes to ten dollars or so. Then they'll let her fiancé win, and the game will be over."

"I see. What do you do on the years when there's no engaged girl to take last place on the stage?" he wondered aloud.

"There's always an engaged couple available. Next year, it will probably be you and Cecily."

Averil didn't know how to respond. Was his enchantment with Cecily so obvious to everyone? Another thought occurred to him. "Indeed? Now, what do you think your sister would say to you if she knew you were making such speculations about her?"

"Tease if you will, but I know my sister's heart." Augusta looked straight ahead and lifted her nose, then tilted her face back toward Averil. "Don't let Cecily fool you. Her height gives her a powerful physical presence, but she's afraid that some men are too proud to look up to a woman—literally. Because she's so tall, she doesn't think she can appear helpless like some of us women pretend to be, so sometimes she's reluctant to be too bold in her speech. A strong woman can be scary to some men, you know."

"I didn't know that." Averil suppressed a chuckle.

Augusta's nose went skyward once again. "I didn't think you would. You seem rather sure of yourself, especially to be so short."

Averil tried not to flinch.

"By that I mean that you don't let anyone intimidate you. And that's a wonderful quality in a man." Augusta nodded, and the look on her face seemed earnest.

Averil grinned. "In that case, thank you." He studied the grove of tall Virginia pines to which they were headed.

"Whatever your future plans with my sister, I know the real reason why you bid on my box. You certainly weren't motivated by any desire to be near me."

Averil tightened his lips and picked up his pace. "If I am that repulsive to you, then perhaps you should decline to lunch with me."

"But your money—"

"Never mind about that. I don't mind making a donation to the school." He stopped walking to give her the opportunity to answer.

Augusta responded with a twirl of her parasol. "My, but if you give up that easily, you'll never win her. Of course I'll lunch with you. It's the least I can do for you. And for her." Her lips formed a slight pout. She took his arm and started walking with a brisk step, keeping her eyes focused on the grove of trees they were rapidly approaching.

Averil felt his heart drop into his shoes. "I'm sorry if this day hasn't gone as you expected. You wanted the young man to win, didn't you?"

"Byron? Never. I've known him too long. He seems more like a brother than a romantic prospect."

"He seemed quite disappointed to lose out on the bid."

"I can't worry about how Byron feels. I have no desire to eat lunch with him today or any other day." Augusta's lips twisted into a remorseful line. "I suppose I sound quite snobbish. I don't mean to. Byron is nice enough, but he's not anyone I'd like as a suitor."

Averil wanted to ask Augusta what special young man had caught her eye, but the question would be much too bold. He opted to try to salvage the situation. "Then at least I saved you from sharing lunch with someone you have no feelings for."

Augusta stared straight ahead and swirled her parasol. "I suppose one could view the outcome in that manner."

Since Augusta continued to act coldly, Averil was pleased when they spotted Cecily and her lunch companion sitting on a blanket beneath the trees. Professor Tobias was sitting close to Cecily. She paid no attention to him. In fact, she seemed to be striving to put as much space between them as she could without appearing rude. Even so, the man sat closer than Averil would have liked.

The contents of the green box were set about. Fried chicken, potato salad, rolls, raw greens, and a jar of iced tea, all looked appealing. The meal he was supposed to be enjoying with Cecily. He wished more than ever he had won the bid.

The smile Cecily aimed in his direction proved to Averil that he had won the prize—at least the only prize that mattered. Or had he? He cringed when he remembered the tall stranger.

Averil tipped his hat to the music teacher, who returned the motion with a scowl. Ignoring the man's obvious though unspoken message, Averil said, "Mind if we join you?"

"Yes," Professor Tobias said. He opened his mouth to say more.

"He means yes, of course we want you to join us." Cecily patted a vacant place on the blanket beside her. "Here. We have plenty of room."

No one disputed Cecily, at least not aloud. As Averil and Augusta sat on the blanket, Professor Tobias's scowl grew deeper. He brought a chicken leg to his lips and bit into it with zest. Augusta remained silent as she sat and opened her boxed lunch. To Averil's delight, its contents proved identical to Cecily's.

"Looks like we both won, eh, Professor Tobias?" Averil

observed. No need to let the man's sour mood spoil the whole lunch.

"The food is excellent," the music teacher muttered in response. "But I thought the idea of the bids was to allow the bachelors to eat alone with their companions."

"You know full well that this was my idea, Professor Tobias," Cecily pointed out. "I really didn't think you'd mind. After all, my sister is among us." Cecily nodded once in Augusta's direction. Augusta's response was to busy herself with distributing the food and keeping the teacups filled.

Averil sensed that Cecily was conveying some sort of unspoken message to her sister. But what? He searched his mind and then remembered. Cecily had mentioned some time ago that Augusta had eyes for their music teacher. He watched the younger Miss Eaton with renewed sympathy. How heartbroken she must have felt! How could she bear to witness such an event? The one who made her swoon bid on her own sister's basket—and won!

Jealousy pricked Averil. He had been so immersed in smoothing Augusta's ruffled feathers that he hadn't thought about his own questions. He wished he'd thought to ask Augusta to identify the tall man who bid on Cecily's box. The way Cecily seemed to be playacting, he had a feeling she wouldn't be forthcoming with the truth about the stranger. Averil resolved to ask Augusta later.

Augusta remained silent throughout most of the meal. She studied her potato salad as though it might contain some secret ingredient and she had been assigned the task of discovering its identity. Occasionally she picked at the small portion of salad and popped a cube of potato in her mouth. Her chicken and rolls remained untouched. When she wasn't concentrating on her food, Augusta peered at her former teacher. Sometimes he would look back at her, but she always averted her eyes too quickly for their gazes to meet.

In the meantime, Cecily chatted brightly as though she had no desire to be anywhere else. Her way of flitting from subject to subject reminded Averil of the way she'd conducted herself in the carriage that morning. This time, however, she kept prodding Augusta, either by touching her on the shoulder or by asking her opinions on certain subjects. Augusta didn't offer much in the way of answers aside from monosyllables and the occasional shrug. Averil began to feel like a character caught up in a drama, although one too hapless to have any control over his own destiny.

The lunch he had so anticipated with Cecily blurred into an image that reminded him of a painting he had seen once by French Impressionist Georges Seurat. The picture was colorful, but the details weren't clear. The swirl of Cecily's chatter, Augusta's busyness with the picnic provisions, and Professor Tobias's aggressive eating, all blended together in a canvas of nebulous detail unfitting for such a lovely spring day. To his surprise, he was glad to see the event come to an end.

He was just as sorry that he had promised Father he'd work that afternoon. He was scheduled to meet the owner of a vacant office building in less than an hour, and he needed time to drive the buggy across the city. He would miss the afternoon's frivolities. Averil supposed he could have argued that his presence at the entire day's festivities would be good for business, but Father was determined that Averil should inspect the empty space before some other tenant snatched it up. Averil had discovered a long time ago that winning an argument with Father about business was an impossibility.

He was grateful when Cecily and Professor Tobias became involved in putting away the remains of their lunch. He took Augusta aside and whispered, "I meant to ask you earlier. Do you know who the tall man who bid on your sister's box was?"

"Tall man?" She thought for a moment. "You must mean Delmar Williams. He and Cecily have had an understanding for years."

"An understanding?"

"Yes, an understanding."

Anxiety bolted through Averil. Cecily had an understanding with someone else? Why hadn't she said anything? And if she really were betrothed to this Mr. Williams, why hadn't he made himself known before now? Averil didn't want to contemplate the possibility. Best to make his exit now.

He extracted his watch from his pocket and made a show of consulting it. "As much as I have enjoyed your company, I'm afraid I must be taking my leave," he announced.

"So soon, Mr. Kingsley?" Cecily asked. "Why, the day seems as though it has barely begun."

"Yes, time does fly when one is engaged in pleasurable pursuits. But my appointment to meet the office landlord is at three o'clock. If I leave now, I'll have just enough time." He looked into Cecily's eyes, which gazed back at him without any hint of guile. "I regret that I cannot see you home."

She nodded, a reaction he expected since this was hardly news to Cecily. They had already made arrangements for her to ride home with her parents. "I understand. Perhaps next time."

*Next time?* She didn't sound like a woman enamored with another man. He searched her eyes for a suggestion of regret and found them filled with emotion. Her look only left him more puzzled. Why hadn't she told him that she was promised to someone else? Doubt gripped his heart. Was everything good about Cecily just a figment of his fertile imagination?

As he left the school grounds, Averil wondered about the new facts he had discovered about Cecily. He realized he didn't know her at all. Certainly she displayed a well-grounded faith and spiritual maturity in Sunday school class. She came from a nice home and a prestigious family. But what else did he know about her? Apparently not enough. Or perhaps too much.

Averil nodded once with determination. He thought he loved

her. His stomach seemed to jump with excitement at the thought. Averil wasn't a man to fall in love easily, and he certainly wasn't one to fall out of love easily.

So what were all these strange feelings? He shook his head, hoping against hope that the motion would clear his brain by shaking out all unwanted and confusing thoughts.

❧

Cecily and Augusta folded the gingham blanket as the music teacher waited. Augusta came toward her, bringing the blanket into a manageable rectangle. She folded the material twice more so that it formed a perfect square. "There. All done."

"Allow me to carry these things to the carriage for you, Miss Cecily," the professor offered.

"That is quite all right," Cecily answered. "I can—"

"Would you, Professor?" Augusta interjected. "I can walk with you." She looked upon the ground as though she realized she might have been too bold. "Since, after all, you might have trouble finding our carriage among all the others here."

Professor Tobias stared at Cecily. His expression indicated he wanted her to intervene, but she refused. "That is an excellent idea, Augusta. I'll go back to the gazebo and meet Mother and Father. You'll be joining us soon?"

"But of course!"

"As much as I would enjoy your company, Miss Augusta, I'm afraid I must be leaving," the music teacher protested.

"Oh?"

"I'm afraid I have a lesson scheduled." No apology displayed itself in his tone. "Another time, perhaps?"

"Another time." The disappointment in Augusta's voice was evident.

Cecily's heart ached for her sister. If only she could offer some sort of balm! But she could not. "Come along, Augusta. Mother and Father await."

Her sister nodded and acquiesced. Cecily had to content

herself with her refusal to acknowledge Professor Tobias's farewell.

They made their way to the gazebo. Neither spoke, their silence indicative of the fact they weren't ready to talk about the day's events.

"There you are, girls!" Mother greeted them as they approached her. "I take it you had a lovely time?"

"Yes, Mother," Cecily answered for them both.

"Cecily!" a male voice called.

Her family turned their heads to see Delmar sprinting across the lawn. The motion of running made him seem more awkward and lanky than usual.

Cecily giggled.

"Now, now, Cecily," Mother admonished. "No need to be rude."

"I know, Mother, but I can't help myself," Cecily explained. "Even you have to admit, he looks a bit odd."

Delmar held onto his hat by placing a hand on top of his head, leaving the other arm to swing to and fro in rhythm with his feet.

"I'll be happy to admit he looks odd. Maybe even odder than usual," Augusta remarked. An amused smile slid onto her countenance.

Mother shushed them as Delmar came within earshot.

"There you are!" He grinned, a sure indication he hadn't heard their conversation, and greeted them. Cecily noted that Mother looked a little too pleased to see Delmar.

"How wonderful that you could be here for the Celebration of Spring!" Mother said in a voice a little louder than necessary.

"I'm delighted I could sneak away from school for a few days," Delmar informed them. "And it's been good to catch up with my old school chums."

"It's good to have you back, Delmar." Father patted him on the shoulder.

"It's good to be back, Sir," Delmar answered. "But I'm afraid my visit will be all too short. I'm due back for examinations next week."

"My, but you've barely gotten off the train, and you'll be getting right back on." Mother clucked in sympathy.

"Early Monday morning," Delmar said. "It's not so bad." He looked at Cecily. "The trip was well worth the effort."

Feeling her cheeks burn, Cecily stared studiously at her feet.

"Might I speak to your daughter for a moment, Mr. Eaton?"

"Why, certainly." Father beamed. "The rest of us will be listening to the band. You can meet us at the gazebo."

Delmar took her by the elbow to lead her behind a large magnolia tree, under which a park bench awaited. Cecily had no desire to appear as though she belonged to Delmar, but she couldn't find a good way to resist without seeming rude. She supposed the obvious lack of enthusiasm she displayed upon seeing Delmar again was impolite enough, but she didn't know what to say.

If he thought her less than mannerly, Delmar acted as though he didn't notice. "I'm sorry I missed out on eating lunch with you."

"I'm sure you didn't lunch alone," answered Cecily.

"No. I ate with my family. Mother sends her regards." He grimaced. "I must admit, I endured a lot of jesting since I failed to win the bid over the music teacher."

Cecily's lips curled. Delmar's brothers were a competitive lot. She could imagine their relentless teasing. "I trust you managed to avoid indigestion all the same." She didn't wait for him to respond to her quip. "At least the students are all winners. Thanks to you and all the other bachelors, we raised more than two hundred dollars for the school."

"Oh?"

Cecily nodded. "That's what Mrs. Baxter told Mother. She's head of the committee this year."

"What a success for her," Delmar remarked. "She outdid Miss Collins."

"And set a high standard for next year's committee chairwoman."

Delmar cleared his throat. "I have to confess, I wasn't thinking of the school while I was trying to win your box. The bidding certainly got hot. If I had known your popularity would grow to such proportions during my absence, I might never have left."

"Don't be ridiculous, Delmar. You know you have to finish school," Cecily insisted. His confirmation about her popularity pleased her, but she was not about to be swayed by flattery. "In fact, I must object to your leaving college to break away for the celebration."

"You leave that worry to me and my professors," Delmar said. "Besides, I wouldn't dream of missing the chance to see you dance around the Maypole."

He motioned for her to take a seat upon the white park bench. Cecily was in no mood to sit and chat with Delmar, especially since his mouth had pressed itself into a severe line. She knew that expression well. Whatever he wanted to talk about, the subject was of some importance and probably not too pleasant.

As always when nerves vexed her, Cecily tried to dissipate the situation with humor. "Now, now. Must we talk about serious matters on such a festive day?" She extended her arm toward the people milling around, listening to the band, eating refreshments, and watching a group of children play tag.

"I must ask, Cecily, when did you become so well acquainted with your music teacher? He used to be the stuff of sport." Delmar sniffed. "Remember when you used to poke fun at his misshapen appearance?"

Cecily cringed. "That was three years ago. Certainly I can be forgiven a lapse or two into meanness. Now, I truly regret any harsh words I said about him."

"Aha!" Delmar lifted a forefinger. "So you have become fond of him."

" 'Fond' is too strong a word. I like him as a music teacher, but beyond that, I am not well acquainted with him. Especially not as a suitor," Cecily defended herself. "In fact, I'm not even his music student anymore."

Delmar's eyebrows rose. "You're not?"

"No. He sent a letter to Father saying that he wanted to discontinue lessons with Augusta but keep me as a student."

"But you and Augusta have been taking lessons from him for years and paying him good money too. Why would he cut off his nose to spite his face unless he's come into a surprise inheritance?"

Cecily pursed her lips together and twirled her parasol. "I'm sure he has plenty of students to fill our places."

"But not his heart, apparently."

"You know fully well I have no interest in Professor Tobias. Augusta happens to be the one—" She clapped her hand over her mouth.

"Augusta? You mean to say she has eyes for the music teacher?" Delmar shook his head and chuckled.

She gave him an imploring look. "You won't say anything, will you?"

"A gentleman never breaks a confidence."

"You always were a gentleman."

"Is that all you can say to recommend me?" His halfway grin belied his serious tone.

Cecily wasn't sure how to answer. If she had harbored any doubt about her feelings for Delmar before this day, seeing him again resulted in its complete dissolution. She liked Delmar well enough, but no matter how much her parents insisted, no matter how tall he was, no matter what his lineage, she didn't love him—even though he had just managed a conversation without once mentioning baseball.

Delmar leaned toward her, but not so closely as to appear improper. Still, Cecily felt like a little mouse trapped in a corner by an imposing tomcat. "You have no idea why I came all the way here from school, do you?"

Cecily swallowed. "To see the Celebration of Spring, I suppose."

"Not entirely. I also came to see you," he said. "I didn't believe Elton when he told me how some door-to-door salesman was pursuing you."

Cecily crossed her ankles. Leave it to Delmar's eldest brother to fill him in on the latest rumors. "I wouldn't say Mr. Kingsley is pursuing me."

Delmar slapped his backbone against the back of the bench and crossed his arms. "So it's true. That little shrimp of a man is nothing but a door-to-door salesman?" An ugly laugh escaped his lips. "In that case, I shouldn't have bothered making the trip."

"Is that so?" Cecily felt anger rise in her chest. "And I'll have you know he's not a shrimp."

"Maybe not to the average girl, but he's certainly a lot shorter than you are."

"But he is mighty in spirit," Cecily retorted.

"Oh, he is, is he?" Delmar's jaw tensed. "In that case, let's send the pastor over to recruit him for the choir. Then you can see him for an hour every Sunday. That's your only hope of seeing him. Because that's all it will ever amount to."

"Why do you say that?"

Delmar looked at the sky, then back at her. "Surely you know your father better than I do. And if there's one thing I know for certain, he would never allow such a person to become a serious suitor for you."

Cecily dug her heels into the ground. "I'll have you know that Mr. Kingsley's company has given him instructions to open a regional office right here in the city." She couldn't resist sharing the good news with Delmar. "Why, at this very moment, he is downtown, inspecting a vacant space. That's the only reason he's not with me now."

"Is that so? I doubt your father would agree with that."

"But—"

Delmar held his palm up in a motion for her to discontinue speaking. "Your father is just being polite. Even I must admit, this Mr. Kingsley fellow made a fair bid on your sister's boxed lunch, and he won the chance to eat with her—and somehow ended up sitting with you and Professor Tobias as well."

Delmar allowed a pause to fill the air, but Cecily didn't respond.

He then added in a patronizing tone, "You certainly can't expect him to see you beyond that."

"Indeed? He escorted me to the festivities."

"Yes. I'm aware of that." The pitch of his voice was so tense that it rose an octave.

"Which is the only reason you made the trip home from school."

"Not the only reason." The usually arrogant Delmar looked at the ground like a shy schoolgirl.

Cecily knew the uncharacteristic gesture was a sure sign he wasn't telling the truth. Her tongue burned with the desire to tell him so, but she managed to quench the urge.

Delmar sighed. "I suppose I have no one to blame but myself for today's unfortunate developments. I should have been more aggressive in my own bidding. Then you wouldn't be harboring such a foolish notion."

Cecily decided to guide the conversational boat to a safe harbor—if only for the moment. "Speaking of my box, how did you know which one was mine?"

He cocked his head. "I asked Augusta, of course."

"Augusta." Cecily nodded. "I should have known. But that doesn't explain how the music teacher knew."

Delmar shrugged. "Maybe he was watching who brought in which box. Or maybe he bribed your cook."

"More likely, he solved the puzzle for himself when he saw you and Mr. Kingsley bidding on my box."

"Could be. Everyone <u>knows</u> we've had an understanding of sorts." Delmar paused and took her hands in his. "Haven't we?"

Guilt shot through her. Had she somehow led him to believe they would one day marry? Her family seemed to think so. Before Averil, she hadn't done much to cause them to think otherwise. "Perhaps we drifted into some sort of arrangement without either of us realizing it." Cecily looked down at her lap.

"I realized it. At least, I thought so."

"Nothing was ever said, and—"

"I know. I blame myself for that as well. I should never have left for school without making our status indisputable." His eyes took on a longing light as his voice softened. "Let's not argue, Cecily. That is the real reason why I came home. I see now that I could lose you. I never should have taken you for granted."

"Delmar—"

"Now, now, I know I haven't been fair to you. If I had made my intentions clear, none of this would have ever happened. So now, I shall." Delmar breathed in audibly and then exhaled. He took her hands in his and looked into her eyes. "Cecily, will you marry me?"

# ten

"What excitement!" Mother proclaimed as the carriage took them home. "Imagine, three gentlemen bidding on our Cecily's box at once. This is a day that will go down in history!"

"I'm afraid you exaggerate, my dear." Father chuckled.

"Three bids on Cecily's box, and nobody but silly old Byron and Mr. Kingsley bid on mine," Augusta muttered. She peered outdoors as if to turn her attention away from the rest of the family.

"Now, now, my sweet," Father consoled. "There will be plenty of time for you to court whatever man strikes your fancy once Cecily is safely married." He turned his twinkling brown eyes to Cecily. "And if events continue to progress as well as they did today at the celebration, that day won't be long in coming!"

"No, indeed!" Mother added, eyes matching the intense sparkle of Father's. "Why, I wouldn't be at all surprised if Delmar didn't decide to speak up after all this time."

"Or perhaps someone else, eh?" Father asked.

Cecily swallowed. Delmar's impromptu proposal had come as quite a shock. She wasn't ready to give him an answer, and she had told him so. Thankfully he didn't seem surprised that she needed more time. Delmar didn't argue with her request that he wait for an answer.

Cecily squirmed under her family's happy scrutiny. She knew if she told them anything at all, they would join forces to help her make a decision. As if she didn't already know their opinions. She suppressed a sigh. She hated keeping secrets from the ones she held most dear. Duplicity wasn't natural to her. Yet the decision was hers to make, and she had promised Delmar she would tell him on the morrow. Her heart beat faster at the thought.

117

She cleared her throat. "Speaking of Delmar, he asked if he could come by tomorrow afternoon after dinner."

"Of course Delmar is welcome in our home any time. But after dinner?" Mother asked. "Why didn't you ask him to join us for dinner? You know he would have been welcome."

"I—I know he would have been welcome. I just didn't think of it at the time."

"That doesn't matter now," Mother said as the carriage pulled into the drive. "Delmar is sure to have many more meals with us in the future." She peered toward Mrs. MacGregor's house. As she eyed the neighbor digging in her flower garden, a self-satisfied smile covered her lips. "I can't wait to tell Gladys what happened today!"

Cecily and Augusta let out small groans. They knew all too well that Cecily's marriage to a member of a prominent family would be a victory for Mother in her rivalry with their neighbor. Mrs. MacGregor's daughter had never been anything to look at, a fact that lessened her prospects so that she didn't marry as well as the MacGregors had hoped. But married she was, and Mrs. MacGregor never let Mother forget that fact.

They watched Mother rush out of the carriage and race toward the MacGregors' garden.

"Oh, no. Once those two get going, that's it. She'll be over there all night," Roger commented. "I might as well see if Jack wants to play a game of catch."

Father agreed. "Fine by me. Be home in time for supper."

"As if Roger would miss supper," Cecily quipped.

"I heard that." Despite his warning tone, Roger exited with a gleeful step.

"Never let it be said Roger learned any manners," Augusta noted. "Doesn't he know ladies always go first?"

"Don't you know sisters aren't the same as ladies?" Cecily asked as she disembarked from the carriage.

"Of course not. Don't you know that?" Augusta joked.

"I suppose not." Standing at her full height, Cecily looked down at her hem and saw that her frock had become wrinkled almost beyond hope. "I'm ready to get out of this dress. It looks about as tired as I feel."

"Me too," Augusta said. "This has been a long day."

The sisters walked along the sidewalk. Upon reaching the wide steps to the verandah, they continued side by side until Cecily allowed Augusta to enter the front door before her. Cecily expected Augusta to be full of the day's news, but she remained silent. As they ascended the curved front stairs together, Cecily noticed that Augusta didn't keep up with her. The skip that was her usual trademark had disappeared from her step.

"What's wrong?" Cecily whispered as they reached the top of the stairs.

Augusta's expression darkened. "You know very well what's wrong."

Cecily tilted her head in the direction of her room. She had a feeling she knew what Augusta wanted to say. "We need to talk. Come on in."

Augusta folded her arms across her chest and followed Cecily into her room. Cecily had barely shut the door behind her when Augusta hissed, "What is the meaning of today?"

"What? I have no idea what you mean."

"Don't try to tell me that. How could you? After everything you said before, how could you turn around and steal Professor Tobias from me like that?" Augusta pouted. Her face turned pink, and her eyes moistened as though tears threatened.

Cecily knew her sister's tactics all too well. She wasn't about to allow babyish behavior to make her feel guilty when she had done nothing wrong. She held up her hand, palm facing Augusta. "Now hold on a minute. I didn't steal him from you."

"Is that so? Then why did you tell him which box was yours?"

"I didn't tell him," Cecily objected.

"Then who did?"

"I wish I knew. Maybe he bribed Cook?" As another idea occurred to Cecily, she snapped her fingers. "More likely, he somehow wormed it out of Roger."

Augusta let out a breath and set her hands at her sides, softening her posture. "Our little brother. I wouldn't be surprised."

"Probably bribed him with a piece of licorice." Cecily noticed the hurt look on Augusta's face. She wished she could say that Professor Tobias had bid on the wrong box, but she knew her sister would never believe such a far-fetched explanation. Not after the way Professor Tobias had acted like a jealous husband when Averil and Augusta joined them for lunch. "I'm so sorry, Augusta. I did everything I could to bring you and Professor Tobias together."

Augusta paused. "I know."

Cecily cringed. "I'm sorry things didn't work out the way you wanted them to." Eager to separate herself from Augusta physically as well as emotionally, Cecily walked over to her vanity and plopped down on the cushioned seat. "Don't you realize that I never once considered Professor Tobias as a romantic prospect—or any prospect, for that matter?"

"But how can that be? He's ever so handsome and romantic." Augusta looked up at the ceiling and clasped her hands to her cheek.

Wondering how the plain Professor Tobias could inspire such fantasies in anyone, Cecily tried not to flinch.

"You don't want to answer, and I know why. You want to spare my feelings." Augusta sent her a doe-eyed look. "Who am I to stand in the way of your love? If you really do want him to court you, I won't object." Her voice was flat, but Cecily knew Augusta meant what she said.

Cecily didn't know how to answer. Her sister's gesture took courage, courage Cecily didn't realize the girl possessed. Truly her baby sister was growing up. "That is so wonderful of you, Augusta, but I meant it when I said I have no interest in him."

Augusta hesitated. "Well, I must admit, I never saw you give him an ounce of encouragement." She sniffled, and then her face shone with a smile that displayed her obvious relief. "So why can't he like me? What's wrong with me?"

"Nothing!" Cecily stood and hurried over to her. She embraced her younger sister as Augusta wailed. She couldn't remember a time when she had felt sorrier for her sister. How much easier it might have been for her if she could think that Cecily had stolen Professor Tobias away from her. Then at least Augusta would have an explanation as to his lack of interest in her. "You don't need to worry about the music teacher," Cecily assured her. "You are beautiful inside and out."

Augusta sniffled again. She looked up at Cecily. "I am?"

Cecily sent Augusta her warmest smile. "Of course you are. Why, you'll have more callers than you can count once I marry."

Augusta broke the embrace, though she didn't move far. The doe-eyed look returned. "How do you know?"

"Didn't Mr. Kingsley bid on your box? And so did Byron."

Augusta placed her hands on her hips. "How do you know Byron bid on my box? You and Professor Tobias had already gone to the pine grove by then."

"I know because Mr. Kingsley mentioned it at lunch." Then Cecily remembered how Augusta pouted all through the meal. "Perhaps you don't remember because you were too busy sulking."

"I suppose I wasn't very pleasant company. Mr. Kingsley hardly got his money's worth from me." She grinned ruefully. "He just bid on my box so he could be near you."

A twinge of guilt shot through Cecily. She almost wished she hadn't told Averil to bid on her sister's box.

"I saw you whispering to Mr. Kingsley after he lost the bid."

"But. . ." Cecily searched for an explanation, but none seemed suitable.

"That's all right. You don't have to lie about it." Augusta chuckled. "You should have seen the distressed look on Professor Tobias's face when you two were talking. He looked as though he wanted to strangle Mr. Kingsley with his bare hands. And Delmar! Why, he turned a thousand shades of crimson!" A sly grin slid over Augusta's lips. "So, what happened when the two of you met after lunch? I know Mother keeps hoping for a marriage proposal."

Cecily didn't answer. She preferred to study the knots in the oak floor.

Augusta lifted her head, took in an audible breath, and clasped her hands to the base of her throat. Her eyes widened and took on an excited light. "Cecily! You don't mean—"

Cecily shook her head. "It's not what you think."

"But he did speak up?"

Cecily didn't want to answer. She ignored her sister's question and stared out of the window.

"It's not like anyone would be surprised," Augusta pointed out. "You and Delmar have an understanding, don't you?"

"That's what everyone says."

Augusta let out a laugh. "Cecily! I think I can read your mind."

Cecily turned to her abruptly. "Can you?"

"Yes. Surely you're not serious about Mr. Kingsley. I know you've been flirting with the idea, but he is nothing more than a handsome stranger, a carpet sweeper salesman. The novelty of him will wear off soon enough, and you'll want to return to the familiar."

"Now you're sounding like Mother."

"Is that such a bad thing?" She paused. "Don't answer that." She filled the room with a melodic laugh. "But you never told me, did he speak up?"

Cecily held up her left hand. "You don't see a ring, do you?"

"Oh." A dark cloud seemed to pass over Augusta's countenance.

"I suppose not. Well, maybe one day. . ."

"Yes." It was Cecily's turn to inspect the ceiling. "I pray that one day the right man will ask."

❧

Averil tried to concentrate on a crossword puzzle, but to no avail. Not wishing to see Cecily that morning, he had done a cowardly thing. He had skipped church. Averil tried to read his Bible during the hour he'd normally be in worship but had met with limited success. Each time he tried to concentrate, he found himself thinking of Cecily. An image of her loveliness popped into his head, whether he was reading the warnings of the prophet Hosea or praises in the Psalms.

"I know I can't avoid church forever, Lord," he muttered aloud. "What dost Thou want me to do?"

The thought of going to another church crossed his mind, but he knew that wasn't the answer. Running away never was. Yet here he sat, in his room, closeted like a hermit. He set down his crossword puzzle on the small table beside his chair and rose to his feet. Averil walked toward the window and peered out. He took passing notice of blooming dogwood trees and lush greenery between the densely packed city houses. He stared with little interest at the occasional carriage that passed on the street below. He watched as children poured into the street to play games, shouting and crying to each other, their voices breaking into the peacefulness of the spring day.

His stomach growled. Had the luncheon hour arrived so suddenly? Then he realized the aroma of baking ham was wafting up the stairs. Perhaps the appetizing smell had spurred his hunger pangs. At least the boardinghouse cook tried to make Sunday dinner an improvement over the usual fare. Still, it couldn't match the food served up at the Eatons'. Or did the food just seem better because of Cecily's company?

"Lord," he pleaded, "why did I make such a rash decision

yesterday? I know I should have gone to church today. Forgive me for making excuses. Forgive my spinelessness."

ىــ

Cecily looked for Averil during worship and Sunday school. Alarm washed over her. Where was he? Could he be ill? He had seemed perfectly fine the day before. She wondered if she should go by the boardinghouse and see about him. She squelched the idea just as quickly. Such a move would be far from proper. Even if she had the nerve to suggest it, neither of her parents would approve. For the time being, she sent up a silent prayer for Averil's health and safety.

Perhaps his absence was for the best. Cecily had to concentrate on Delmar, and if Averil were anywhere near, she wouldn't be able to think of anyone—or anything—else. Delmar had promised to appear at the Eatons' after the noon meal. Cecily dreaded the moment of his arrival. What could she possibly say to him? When he'd proposed marriage the day before, she had wanted to blurt out a resounding no. Delmar wouldn't hear of it. Perhaps he was right. Perhaps sleeping on it was best. She knew her answer would be in the negative all the same.

The Lord's admonition to honor one's mother and father rang through her head. "Lord, would I be dishonoring them by refusing Delmar's proposal of marriage? I know how much Mother wants me to marry him." Then she remembered that Father wasn't as encouraging. If her parents weren't of like mind on the subject, no wonder she was so confused.

Or was she? Delmar was upstanding and certain to make a good husband, but being near him didn't make her heart flutter the way it did when she was anywhere near Averil. Yet what did she know about Averil? Next to nothing. He wasn't from her hometown, nor did she know anything about his family. Of course in the end, she wouldn't be marrying his family. She would be marrying him.

"Stop it!" The sound of her voice startled her. She hadn't meant to utter her thought aloud.

How had she jumped from thinking of Averil as a pleasant companion and someone she wanted to learn more about to a serious suitor? The beating of her heart betrayed her. How could she have fallen in love so suddenly?

# eleven

Opportunities for fellowship and chitchat abounded at Miss Hallowell's boardinghouse every day, but Averil was in no mood to socialize. He had tired of pretending to care about the older boarders' aches and pains. The last time Mr. Rose approached him for conversation, Averil had to hold his tongue to keep himself from debating politics.

Regardless of the subject, he had wearied of talking. Some days on the job, as he traveled from street to street, knocking on every door, he felt as though his mouth stayed in constant motion. No matter how enthusiastic he felt about his product, repeating the virtues of the Capital Duster Electric Pneumatic Carpet Renovator grew tiresome by late afternoon. Keeping his voice strong and confident, as though his last customer were his first and he hadn't already delivered his pitch twenty times that day, could be a strain. Maintaining a smile on his face that was neither too broad nor too weak proved a challenge. Every day he resolved to give his future sales staff an increase in commission.

He opened his book, a large tome written by the historian Josephus. He felt a smile cover his face, a sincere one this time. With a pleasant exhalation of breath, he welcomed the solitude of his small room and the opportunity to read without interruption.

"Mr. Kingsley!" Miss Hallowell screeched. His landlady's voice carried easily from the bottom of the stairs.

Averil let out a slight groan. He noticed by the clock on his desk that dinnertime was nearing. Surely Miss Hallowell wasn't calling him to dinner this early. In the weeks he had been a boarder in her house, that had never happened. Dinner was served at five o'clock on the dot, never deviating from the appointed time. Sometimes she asked her male boarders for help with minor repairs, but never by shouting from the parlor to the rooms above. What could she possibly want with him?

He clapped his book shut and laid it on the bed. Perhaps he could return to his reading later that night before retiring for a good night's sleep.

"Mr. Kingsley!" she called again.

Apparently the matter was urgent. In compliance, he made a hasty exit from his room and hurried to the top of the stairs.

"Yes, Miss Hallowell?" he answered in a voice that he hoped was loud enough for her to hear, but soft enough to be considered gentlemanly.

"You have a long-distance telephone call!" she shouted.

*A long-distance telephone call?*

"Oh!" He ran down the steps.

A telephone call! Averil had chosen Miss Hallowell's boardinghouse partly because it boasted the luxury of a telephone. He relished the knowledge that he could reach his father quickly should urgent business need to be conducted. Father agreed. The call could only be from him. Some of Averil's friends were corresponding with him by letter, but none of them would have news to share that was urgent enough to warrant such an expense. The thought reminded him that, eager to squeeze every last drop of value out of every penny, Father wouldn't be happy should Averil keep him waiting.

From the corner of his eye, Averil noticed his fellow boarders watching him with intense curiosity. A long-distance call was as rare in the house as Christmas. He had become an oddity indeed.

Mr. Rose shuffled his newspaper, turning the page to show he would be too busy reading to overhear anything being said on Averil's end. Miss Henton increased the speed of her knitting.

At the rate the red sleeve began to grow from a ball of yarn, her nephew's sweater was liable to be finished by supper. Mrs. Pimm looked up from writing her letter. She dipped her pen into the inkwell, then began scratching more words upon cream-colored paper. All this busyness, entered into to conceal the fact they were listening, was bound to result in his affairs becoming common knowledge among all the boarders. The ones not present were certain to get a briefing from those who pretended total immersion in their individual pursuits.

Only Miss Hallowell didn't bother with pretense. She handed the receiver to Averil and retrieved the tablecloth, dishes, and utensils from the sidebar. He watched as she slipped a well-worn but clean white cloth over the oak table. As she set the table, she kept her head cocked so that one ear was always open to what was being said. For the hundredth time, Averil resolved to leave the boardinghouse by the end of the month.

Averil turned away from her. He picked up the candlestick receiver and spoke. "Hello?"

"Are you Mr. Averil Kingsley?" a female voice inquired.

"Yes."

"Hold for the connection to your party." The operator paused. "All right, then. Go ahead, Sir."

Father's voice burst onto the line. "Averil? Is that you, my boy?"

*My boy?* He never called Averil by that name unless he was pleased. "Yes, Father. It's me."

"Good to hear your voice again. From what you write in your letters, it sounds like they're treating you pretty well down there in Virginia."

Averil glanced toward the dining room table. "Yes, they are. Miss Hallowell's cook is preparing one of my favorites tonight. Fried fish." He flashed a grin toward his landlady, who smiled and nodded in return.

"Scrod?"

"Trout, I believe."

Miss Hallowell's face beamed with a wide smile as she nodded with vigor.

"That's mighty fine. Mighty fine," Father confirmed. "I'm calling about the office space you looked at yesterday. What did you think? Was it fine enough for the Capital Duster Company to call a regional office?"

"I thought the rent was reasonable," Averil said. "The space was more than adequate and well maintained. Not to mention, the location is in a prime spot on Broad Street." He paused and waited for an answer. Averil clenched his teeth. His parent was certain to ask him to look at other properties, perhaps less expensive ones. If he did, Averil wasn't sure how he could respond. The one he saw yesterday was the best he had visited.

"Broad Street, eh? That sounds even better than I first thought."

"It was the best suite of offices I've seen for the money." Despite the confidence his voice indicated, Averil braced himself for an argument.

"Well, then, if you're satisfied, so am I."

"Really?"

Father chuckled. "You seem surprised. Did you expect me to dispute your word?"

"No, Sir," he blurted out before thinking. "I mean, well, I thought perhaps you would want me to see more properties before making a final decision."

"Not if you're happy with this one. Besides, you don't have all week to tarry looking at offices. You've got to get out and sell our machines, my boy," Father reminded him. "Now, why don't you notify the landlord—Orwell Smythe, was it?"

"Yes."

"Notify Mr. Smythe that we're ready to sign a one-year lease," Father instructed. "Tell him he'll be getting his deposit and first month's rent within the week. And you can go ahead with hiring a secretary and another salesman, if you want. Once we get a

Capital Duster Electric Pneumatic Carpet Renovator in every fine home in Richmond, we'll need to expand."

"Yes. To Petersburg. And then maybe to Norfolk."

"You'll be surprised how fast you'll move. Why, Capital Duster will be known all over the state in the next two or three years. And if you play your cards right, all over the Mid-Atlantic Region within five."

"Just in time to introduce our next model."

"That's right," Father agreed. "Then you can start all over again, selling new machines to everyone. You have learned your lessons well."

"I do my best."

"In fact, I'm feeling generous today. If you think you can handle the load, why not hire two good salesmen?"

"I could, but I was hoping you'd send someone down from the home office," Averil revealed. "If you want to know the truth, I thought perhaps Joe Conners might be interested in the position."

"Joe Conners? No, my boy. I'm not giving up my best salesman. Not even for you. Besides," he said, his voice softening, "you need to start just like I did. From the ground up. Build your own sales force. Use people you know and trust."

"But I don't know anyone—"

"It's only a matter of time before you will." He paused. "If you think I'm being unreasonable, don't. Your grandfather didn't hand me everything on a silver platter, and that's why I can be proud of my accomplishments today. I can call them my own. Understand?"

"I understand." And he did, all too well. "You have a point, as usual, Father."

"Of course I do," Father said. "If I didn't have confidence that you could do this job and do it well, I wouldn't trust you with the responsibility."

Averil nodded before he remembered that Father couldn't see

him over the telephone. "Thank you, Father." His heart swelled with pride upon finally receiving hard-won compliments from his father.

"Son, you've done a tremendous job selling the Capital Duster Electric Pneumatic Carpet Renovators since you've been in Richmond. I have already received letters from two of your customers. They wrote me to say how pleased they are with our machines and what a fine salesperson you are," said Father.

Averil gasped. "People have written to you? I had no idea." He searched his memory to try to ascertain who among his customers would take the time to write to the company. He came up empty. "But who?"

"Who? Let me see." Averil heard Father riffling through papers. "One letter is signed by Mr. and Mrs. Alvin Johnson."

"Yes." Averil pictured an older man with a thin frame and thinner hair and a mousy little wife. Mr. Johnson had dominated the transaction, while his wife had remained mute. He had seemed grumpy, complaining about the cost of the machine, asking for free attachments, and insisting that Averil visit him again in six months to be sure the machine was performing satisfactorily. Apparently Averil and the carpet renovator had won over the Johnsons.

Averil heard paper rattling once more.

"Let's see here," Father said. "The second is from a Miss Warner."

"I remember her as well." The lively brunette's letter came as less of a surprise. Miss Warner had been a tad on the flirtatious side. He would have to be careful around her. Still, he made a mental note to stop by the Johnsons' and Miss Warner's the next day to chat about their new machines. Might as well try to live up to the good impression he had already made. References, especially from the locals, were always a plus in the sales business.

"I'm glad to hear that you remember your customers," Father

said. "That's always important in our line of business."

"Aren't you surprised anyone bothered to write?" Averil ventured.

"Of course not. We get letters all the time. I suppose you just hadn't been privy to them since you never worked in the front office. Miss Benton always answers them. And if things continue as they have, your secretary will be quite busy answering customer letters in the future."

"I hope so."

Father cleared his throat. "People get rather emotional about the machines they use to clean the house, don't you know? They seem like part of the family after awhile. Now you keep on telling everybody what a wonderful carpet renovator we make, and you continue to follow up with your customers, just like you're doing. Keep on, and before you know it, one day you'll be able to step back and say you can't remember the day when the Capital Duster Company wasn't a welcome fixture in the city."

"Thank you, Father." Averil swallowed. Finally he had earned his father's approval and praise!

Averil heard his mother's voice in the background.

"Your mother sends her regards," Father said. "She'll be writing you a letter this week, as usual. Now then, you wrote about meeting a girl? Tell me about her. A Miss Cecily Eaton, you say?"

"Yes." He opened his mouth to protest that he was not seeing Miss Eaton when Father interrupted.

"I happened to mention the Eatons to Boswell the other day. You remember him."

Averil groaned inwardly. Did the whole state of New York have to know about his social life? "Yes I do. I believe he's the one who suggested we break into this market."

"You remember. Good. That quality will come in useful during your career, let me assure you. Anyway, Boswell knows the Eatons. He says they're a fine family. With a recommendation like that, I'm certain your mother and I would approve heartily of Miss Eaton."

Despite his father's glowing words, Averil cringed. It was just like him to nose around, trying to find out all he could about his son's new acquaintances in Richmond, be they business or personal.

"Have you asked her father about courting her yet?" Father wanted to know.

Averil felt another inward groan. "I escorted her to the Celebration of Spring festivities, but I'm afraid she's rather popular. I didn't know it when I agreed to escort her, but she's practically engaged."

"Practically engaged? Balderdash. That's not the same as 'already married.' If you want the girl, don't let a little thing like an engagement stop you."

"Father! You can't be serious."

"But I am. All's fair in love and war." Though Averil couldn't see him, he imagined Father was lifting his forefinger toward the crown molding on the parlor ceiling.

"What about honor?" Averil asked.

"Honor? You can't eat, drink, or marry honor, my boy. You need the right woman by your side if you want to be a success in this life. Isn't that right, my dear?"

"That's right." He heard Mother answer in the background.

"You are a Kingsley!" Father reminded Averil. "If this girl is the one you really want, you go over there and make known your intentions. That is, if she is really worthy of bearing the Kingsley name."

"She is, Father. But I haven't been in the city that long—"

"Never waste a moment! That's what I always say. If I had, I never would have gotten your dear mother."

He could hear his mother laugh. The sound of her voice made him happy and homesick at the same time. "Tell Mother I miss her."

"She knows. But she's happy, knowing you're making a name

for yourself where you are. I'm not retiring anytime soon, you know," Father assured him.

"I know."

"When that day comes, you can move back here if you like." He paused. "Or you can make the Richmond office our corporate headquarters."

"Corporate headquarters! But we've always been based in New York."

"Yes, but a new century has dawned. Progress, you know. Progress," Father said. "And of course, our company is a big part of that. Without us, women might still be forced to beat their rugs over the clothesline."

Averil doubted the truth of such a sweeping assessment, but decided not to express his opinion.

Not that Father noticed. "And speaking of the new office," he continued, "are you ready to get out of that boardinghouse and get yourself a real place you can call home?"

Averil looked around the dining room, with its long oak table and simple chairs. No chair rail or crown molding adorned the plain walls, although a bell pull with an array of flowers that he imagined Miss Hallowell had stitched some time ago added interest near the doorway. Chintz curtains decorated large windows—a far cry from the heavy brocaded and velvet window dressings he knew at home. For a boardinghouse, it was respectable and well kept enough, but nothing like where he imagined living for any length of time.

"When I first arrived here, I had no idea I'd succeed to the point you'd open an office here," Averil admitted. "I thought I'd be returning home. So I never gave much thought to where I'd live permanently."

"Well, start thinking in terms of a permanent place there. And to facilitate that, I'll be giving you a salary of forty-five dollars a week, and you'll be known as the president of the Mid-Atlantic Division."

A raise and a title! What more could he ask? Then Averil

remembered how much Father liked a tough negotiator. "How about fifty dollars a week?"

Averil had forgotten that his conversation was taking place where his fellow boarders could hear. He could almost hear their necks snap as they whipped their heads in his direction. Since Miss Hallowell's wasn't the most luxurious or the most expensive boardinghouse in the city, any mention of money caused ears to perk up. Averil swivelled and faced the parlor and witnessed several pairs of eyes upon him.

Embarrassed, he turned away. By default, the motion caused him to see straight into the dining room. Miss Hallowell was setting the knives around the plates. Her pursed lips and downward cast indicated her unhappiness. She must have conjectured that such a sum would be causing her to lose a boarder—a boarder who rented one of the better rooms and who always paid his rent on time.

"That's my boy!" Father was saying on the other end of the line. "Never accept the first offer. Fifty dollars a week it is." He chuckled. "You know, I might have gone as high as fifty-five dollars if you had asked."

"I know better than that, Father."

He chortled. "You've got me there, my boy. You've up and gotten pretty smart on me. I can see you will manage our new regional office very well."

"Thank you. I'll do my best." He turned toward the wall. "That's mighty generous of you."

"Of course it is. I'm a generous man. And speaking of generosity, this telephone call is costing me money," Father said. "Lots of money. Not only is the phone company getting rich, but also I'm paying you forty-five, no, fifty dollars a week. Now, rest today and then prepare for a productive week, my boy. You have much to do to ensure the continued success of the Capital Duster Company. I'll wire the rental monies to the Western Union office in the Jefferson Hotel tomorrow morning."

"Yes, Sir. Thank you for calling, Father. Good-bye."

After he hung up, Averil sighed. He faced the open window and vaguely noticed clouds gathering in the sky, but he paid them no attention. His mind was too much upon his family. He couldn't remember the last time his father had been so complimentary. He recalled when he had left New York, stepping on the train to come to Richmond. Doubt had clouded Father's face. Mother sniffled into her handkerchief. His brother-in-law looked arrogant as always, determined to run the New York operation himself. Averil had even doubted his own abilities. What if he had come all this way just to fail? What if he had been forced to return home, heir to the company but answering to his father and brother-in-law for the rest of his days? He shuddered.

*I thank Thee, Lord, for giving me the courage and tenacity to succeed here in a place I didn't know, among strangers, and against all the predictions of my family back home.*

"Bad news?" Miss Hallowell interrupted.

"No. Why would you think that?"

"Your eyes were closed for a second, like you were prayin'."

"I was praying."

"Then it was bad news."

Averil chuckled. "I pray whether I get bad news or good. It's just as important to talk to God when times are good as when times are bad, don't you think?"

Miss Hallowell shrugged. "I hate to bother the Lord unless I've got somethin' real important to say."

"All of your concerns—and praises—are important to Him."

"Whatever you say. So, are you goin' to tell me what the news was or just give us a sermon?"

"I think I'll stop with the sermon."

"What?" The look on her face was so comical that Averil couldn't resist laughing.

"All right. I'll tell you. You have a right to know, anyway. As you probably guessed from my end of the conversation—"

"You mean the end where you just kept agreein' with everything he said?"

He resisted the urge to reprimand her for nosiness. After all, the telephone was located in a boardinghouse dining room, a place where one could hardly expect complete privacy. "I saw no need to argue with my father."

"I understand." She nodded and wiped a fork on her apron. "I know what it's like to have strong parents."

Averil decided to ignore her last observation. "I've been instructed by my fath—I mean, employer, to seek more permanent accommodations soon."

He decided to escape up the stairs where he would be away from prying eyes, curious looks, and expressions of concern. For the first time in years, Averil felt as though he was a success in his profession. If only the rest of his life were in such good order. Father's encouragement about Cecily only served to make him feel more depressed. So many good things were happening in his life—opening the regional office, his father's newfound confidence in him—but he had no one close by with whom to share his triumph. Life in Richmond, no matter how victorious, could only be bittersweet without the woman he had grown to love.

If only he had asked Mr. Eaton if he could court Cecily before she had come to an understanding with Delmar! Then he would stand a chance.

# twelve

As the family was finishing their Sunday dinner of roast beef, Cecily heard the clopping and clacking of horses' hooves approaching their house. The sound was merely the culmination of a meal Cecily hadn't been able to enjoy. For the umpteenth time, she dug her fork into a small mound of creamed potatoes and swirled it back and forth as she stared at her half-empty plate.

Augusta touched her shoulder. "Don't just sit there. It's got to be Delmar!"

*Of course it's Delmar. No one else would be visiting. Unless. . .*

Augusta jumped up from the table and rushed into the parlor. A moment later, Cecily heard her voice all the way to the back of the house. "He's here!"

*Delmar. I wish it were Averil.*

Father gulped down the last bit of his coffee and slid back the substantial chair at the head of the table. "I suppose it's my fatherly duty to greet him."

"Thank you, Father." Cecily knew the tone of her voice hardly matched the excitement in her sister's.

As Augusta returned to the dining room, Mother said, "I do believe the whole city knows that Cecily has a gentleman caller. Really, Augusta, you must learn to restrain yourself." She pointed to Augusta's plate. "Now sit down and finish your meal."

Augusta nodded and complied, though she wore a slight pout.

Cecily was in no mood to finish her potatoes. She placed the napkin against her lips and then set it in her lap. "May I be excused from the table, Mother?"

"Certainly. No need to keep him waiting." She beamed.

"Especially not when this visit may be the start of an extremely bright future for you both."

"Yes, Mother." Cecily placed her soiled napkin beside her plate and rose from her mahogany chair.

"Now, now. You must show more enthusiasm than that." Mother jumped up from her seat. "Here, let me look at you." She surveyed Cecily from the top of her chignon to the tip of her kid leather Sunday shoes. She nodded in approval. "Yes, your Sunday dress looks quite well on you. Rose always was your best color."

Cecily nodded, even though her stomach felt as though it had twisted into a tight knot. She hated to disappoint anyone, and she knew she was on her way to upsetting not only Delmar, but Mother as well.

The knot tightened when she recalled Averil's absence that morning in church. She had looked over her shoulder more than once, anticipating his arrival. He never materialized. He had seemed the picture of robust health the day before. Surely he hadn't contracted some sort of illness to keep him away from worship. An unwelcome pang of guilt shot through her clenched stomach. Had she somehow offended Averil? Had she scared him off or had someone else? Or was she imagining things because of her own conflicting feelings?

Perhaps his absence was for the best. If he had been in her Sunday school class, how could she have avoided inviting him to Sunday dinner, as had become her custom?

She sent up a silent prayer, one of many she had prayed since the end of the Celebration of Spring.

*Heavenly Father, I know my heart, and I know how Thou art leading me. I understand that nothing with Averil is certain and that I may be misreading Thy divine will and plan for my life. If I am mistaken, Lord, guide me in accepting Delmar's proposal of marriage.*

"Now," Mother interrupted, "I'm sure your father has had

ample time to greet Delmar. Why don't you go on in the parlor? You and Delmar can talk. After a bit, I'll send in a piece of cherry pie and cup of tea for each of you. How does that sound?"

"As if you would let me argue." Cecily smiled. She heard Father and Delmar talking in the parlor.

"I think they've had enough time to greet one another. Now would be the perfect time for you to make your entrance," Mother prodded.

Cecily wished she could think of an excuse to linger in the safety of the dining room, but none came to mind. She nodded a weak acquiescence and left.

Augusta greeted her in the hallway. She touched Cecily on the shoulder and whispered, "This is so exciting! Delmar is here to propose marriage. I just know it!"

Not knowing how else to respond, Cecily nodded slowly.

"So it's true! He's going to propose! Mother and Father will be so happy, Cecily," Augusta assured her. "They'd both much rather see Delmar join the family than. . ."

Augusta's near admission caused Cecily's stomach to lurch. Perhaps she was about to make the biggest mistake of her life.

"You look mighty peaked. Why, you are going to accept, aren't you?" Augusta's eyes widened as her hand flew from Cecily's shoulder to her mouth.

Cecily opened her lips to speak, but no words came out.

Augusta clenched both of Cecily's forearms. "If he asks, you've just got to accept! You've just got to!"

"Why?"

"Because!" Augusta shook her head in obvious exasperation. "You don't want to be a. . .a spinster!" Her voice lingered on the word "spinster" as though it were the equivalent of an untimely death.

Cecily swallowed. In some ways, spinsterhood did seem like a form of death. Death to so many possibilities. Death to the idea of the love of a husband, to the comforts of children.

"Do you?" Augusta pressed.

She still couldn't answer right away. The thought that she might be alone for the rest of her days had never occurred to Cecily. She contemplated for a moment what life might be like as a dutiful spinster daughter and later as a beloved maiden aunt to the children Augusta and Roger were certain to have one day.

"There are worse fates," she concluded aloud. "If God does not wish for me to marry, I shall live my life as a single woman."

Augusta grimaced. "I doubt you really want to be a spinster. And if you know what's good for you, you'll grab the brass ring, or should I say, the engagement ring." She giggled at her attempted humor. Just as quickly, her grin melted and she gasped. "Unless Mr. Kingsley has already spoken up."

"No." Cecily's heart beat more rapidly at the thought.

"Oh." Augusta looked at the floor, then back up into Cecily's face. "That's all for the best, then. You know Mother would never approve of a mere salesman."

"But—"

"Even if he is in charge of a regional office." Augusta placed a forefinger on Cecily's shoulder. "You know what they say. Never count your chickens before they're hatched." She tilted her head toward the parlor. "You've got certainty in Delmar. Not so with Mr. Kingsley."

"Thank you for your good advice," Cecily answered in a tone that her sister would know conveyed the opposite. Eager to escape, she brushed past Augusta and made her way to the small room in the front of the house.

"Ah, there is my dear Cecily now." Father rose from his wing chair. Cecily noticed his voice seemed more cheerful and loud than necessary.

Following Father's lead, Delmar rose from his position on the brocaded sofa. A cocksure grin covered his face. "You look lovely today, Cecily."

"Yes, she does." Father glanced at Cecily with pride. "Well now. I know you two don't need me around. You enjoy your visit. We'll be in the kitchen, Cecily." He nodded and exited before either Cecily or Delmar could respond.

Cecily wished Father could have stayed. Even though she had known Delmar since they were both barely able to talk, she suddenly felt awkward and shy. She didn't want to sit directly beside him on the sofa. Before Delmar could suggest a seat, Cecily slid into the chair just vacated by Father. She looked into Delmar's face with a smile that she knew had to seem contrived. Delmar twitched his lips and repositioned himself on the sofa without comment.

Cecily hoped Delmar wouldn't hesitate to address the reason for his visit, but she soon discovered she was to be disappointed. He leaned back into the cushions and waxed on about the sermon preached at his church during worship that morning. Cecily made certain not to linger in any discussion concerning Sunday school class. The temptation to mention Averil's absence might be too much to resist.

Fortunately for Cecily, Delmar didn't show any interest in the happenings at Cecily's church. "Yes, a fine sermon is just what we need after a long day of festivities such as the ones we enjoyed yesterday."

At last they were getting closer to the topic that laid heavily on her mind.

"Yes, indeed." Cecily's heart lurched with pleasure and excitement as she remembered sharing lunch with Averil.

"Of course, getting carried away in all the fuss and commotion is not uncommon," Delmar observed.

"Fuss and commotion? But I thought the event was quite well run and pleasurable. Did you see anyone act untoward?"

"Of course not. You should know the school attracts only the finest and most upright young gentlemen and prominent families. It always has and always will." His chest puffed up.

"After all, it is my alma mater."

"As I am aware."

"Even so, yesterday certainly was exciting." Delmar paused. "Take the bidding on the boxed lunches, for example."

Cecily could feel her heart beating. "Yes. That was exciting."

"The fact that three different men bid on your box certainly was extraordinary." Delmar leaned toward her.

"I don't know. I think that has happened several times in the past." Cecily racked her brain in search of an example, but she couldn't recall one.

"Perhaps. Although not to a lady of your station, I'm sure." He set his backbone against the cushion and crossed his arms. The steel glint in his eye reminded her of how a schoolmaster must view a mischievous little boy.

She knew the only way to face Delmar was with a show of backbone. "Are you saying ladies of my station are not supposed to be popular?"

"They are not supposed to be flirtatious enough to be that popular." Delmar raised his eyebrows. "If I didn't know you to be an upstanding Christian woman, I would have been truly horrified."

"Is that so?" The conversation was taking a strange direction Cecily could not have anticipated. She decided to weigh each word with care. "I'm not sure I like what you seem to be implying. Certainly I misinterpret what you intend to say."

Rather than issuing the apology she expected, Delmar formed his mouth into a severe line. "Since we spoke yesterday, I have been thinking quite a lot about the bidding and what it says about you. I know you are quite sheltered, which is a fine thing for a lady from a good and respectable family. I realize you are not acquainted with the ways of, shall we say, ladies who are not quite so respectable. Since your father apparently has not broached the subject, it has become my duty to inform you." He paused. "Ladies of your breeding don't generally encourage three suitors at once."

Cecily laughed in spite of herself. "You accuse me of encouraging three suitors? I did no such thing. The idea is utterly preposterous."

"Indeed? Doth thou protest too much?"

"One must protest vehemently when faced with a false charge. I'll have you know that I have no idea at all what possessed Professor Tobias to bid on my box."

"What about the other man? The salesman?" Delmar asked. "He tried to sell my mother one of those newfangled carpet sweepers last week, but she declined to purchase one." Delmar sniffed as though his mother had won a great victory.

"Too bad for her. My mother purchased one, and so did Mrs. MacGregor next door. I'm sure both of them will be quite pleased with their machines. In fact, they are in such high demand, the factory is barely able to keep up with all the orders." She couldn't resist a self-satisfied smile. "But you needn't worry. As soon as your mother changes her mind, she'll have plenty of opportunity to buy one herself."

"So he plans to swoop down on the city from time to time from wherever it is he comes so he can visit each home more than once?" Delmar quipped.

"That won't be necessary. I understand that Mr. Kingsley will be establishing a regional office here in the city soon. He is apparently very important in his company." Cecily heard the pride in her voice.

"Is that so? Then why is he still selling carpet sweepers door to door?"

Cecily didn't have a good answer. "I. . .um. . .I suppose he's in the process of hiring other people to help him."

"I see," Delmar said as though he didn't see at all. "Regional office or not, I'm sure your parents are appalled by the very notion of such a person attempting to buy the pleasure of your acquaintance at the festival, whether you are amenable to the idea or not. It's a shame, really, that the practice of bidding, however old-fashioned and charming, leaves our young women vulnerable to the likes of such carpetbaggers, carpet-sweeper salesmen, or whatever you care to call them. I realize your parents always do what is right and proper. Of course they couldn't keep that man from bidding on your box or on your sister's. And naturally, since he won lunch with her, she was obligated to carry out the promise to dine with him. But after that fiasco, I'm sure you set him straight on the matter that you are not available to new suitors. You do realize, Cecily, that the Celebration of Spring's events could lead to a great scandal."

"I don't see how. I have done nothing wrong." She tried to keep her voice even, although her anger simmered.

"I know you didn't do anything wrong intentionally. But as I said, a lady of good breeding would never let herself be pursued by three suitors at once. Especially not in public."

Cecily tapped her fingers on the arm of the chair. "And just what do you think I could have or should have done? Do you think I would have appeared more ladylike had I jumped off the platform, waved my arms in the air, and shouted for the bidding to stop?"

"Perhaps not," Delmar had to admit. "But lesser events, even when all parties involved were above reproach, have led local tongues to wag in the past. And certainly the Eaton name should not be besmirched by gossip and rumor. I must tell you, when I first arrived home last evening, I almost regretted having asked you to marry me. I'm afraid the question was posed rather impetuously, without much forethought."

"Really? I was led to believe that you had been planning to ask me for years," she couldn't resist observing.

Delmar cleared his throat. "Just not at that particular moment in time."

Cecily doubted him, but decided not to contradict his word. "You said 'almost.' You only 'almost' regret asking me?" She felt her mouth twist into a rueful line.

His smile was bittersweet. "I spoke too hastily. I really don't regret asking you, not for a moment. In fact, I'm willing to announce our engagement after my school term ends next month. That should rescue your family name from any hint of tarnish."

Cecily didn't answer right away. She feared she would say something she would later regret. How dare Delmar act as though he were granting her a huge indulgence! She wondered if he really wanted to marry her at all. She could hear the teakettle whistling from the kitchen. She felt as hot as the boiling water but kept her steaming rage contained.

"I have a splendid notion," he continued, obviously not observing Cecily's doubtful expression. "Your father can host an elaborate engagement party. We will announce our betrothal then. Perhaps we can even announce a set date. A Christmas wedding would be nice. Don't you agree?" He didn't wait for Cecily's answer. "We'll be the toast of the city. Surely a large party will take everyone's mind off yesterday's unfortunate events."

"Do you really believe that?"

"You know how the public eats up anything on the society pages." He nodded his head toward her and raised his eyebrows. "You're an Eaton. You know as well as I that any lavish event with members of our two families as principles is certain to cause quite a stir. Everyone who is anyone will be invited, and the rest of the city will read all about us in the society pages. We are sure to be celebrated."

Cecily couldn't argue that what Delmar said was true. "Would you be as eager to rescue my name from tarnish if my family wasn't prominent?"

Delmar dug his heel into the rug. "Why. . .why. . . ," he stammered. "I'm sure I would."

"Really?" Sarcasm dripped from her voice.

He bristled. "Now it is my turn to say that I'm not sure I like what you seem to be implying."

"Fine, then. I'll make everything crystal clear. I believe you harbored very little interest in me until yesterday."

His mouth dropped open. "Now wait just a minute—"

"Allow me to finish." She paused. "I do believe you took for granted that we had some sort of unspoken understanding. I can't say I lay all the blame for that at your feet. Members of my own family were all too eager to believe our marriage was inevitable. However, you showed no enthusiasm about courting me until yesterday when the other men started bidding on my box."

"But I've been away at school." His voice rose in pitch, a sure sign that he was searching for a defense.

"It's not as though you pursued me with any ardor before you left."

"That's not true!" he protested. "I escorted you to plenty of places."

"If you call meeting me at the event and then leaving separately 'escorting' me, then I suppose you could say that." Cecily shook her head.

"Are you saying I have been anything less than a gentleman toward you?"

"Never."

"That's what I thought." He lifted his nose in the air.

Cecily tried not to wrinkle her own nose in response. Delmar's attitude told her that he worried more about his name and reputation than her feelings. She wanted to tell him so, but decided nothing would be accomplished by enjoying a vigorous debate. "Don't worry, Delmar. None of this is your fault. In fact, I'm glad it happened. Now we know once and for all that we aren't meant to be."

"I never said that."

"But I just did. If I had any doubts before this weekend commenced, I have no doubt now. I have been praying ever since you proposed. I don't feel the Lord leading me to accept."

"Did you feel His prodding before I arrived today?"

"No. I prayed about it all evening and much of the morning."

"In that case, you got your answer mighty quickly." He stared into her eyes. "Or is it more likely that Mr. Kingsley's attentions have distracted you?"

"If you were the man for me, nothing Mr. Kingsley could do would ever keep us apart," she said in all truthfulness. "I'm sorry, Delmar. There is nothing more to say." She arose from her seat to dismiss him.

"Very well." Delmar lifted his nose in the air as he rose from the sofa. "In that case, I'm sure your sister will welcome my attentions."

"My sister?" Cecily stood to her full height. She felt a surge of anger flood her face with heat.

"Now who's jealous?" Delmar didn't conceal his feeling of victory from his voice or pleased expression.

"No, indeed. Your quick dismissal of me and willingness to move on so quickly only serve to prove my point. It seems as though you had this all planned out. If I turned you down, you would simply move on to my sister. Your motive is a match with an Eaton rather than any desire to spend the rest of your life with me, as a person."

"Think what you will." Delmar's voice was dismissive.

His cavalier attitude only served to stoke her ire. "I'll be certain to pass my feelings on to Augusta."

"You are at liberty to do so. But the final decision is hers alone."

Before Cecily could answer, the maid entered the room with a tray containing two cups of tea and two slices of cherry pie.

"I would suggest that you stay for dessert," Cecily said, "but I'm afraid I've lost my appetite."

# thirteen

Cecily watched as Delmar slowly crossed the verandah, lumbered down the seven steps to the green lawn, and began his journey along the curved brick walkway to his waiting buggy. She waited for a feeling of regret. The tugging at her heart didn't come. Instead, her sense of relief grew with each step he put between them.

She did not feel alone. Jesus was with her in spirit, holding her elbow, leading her along in life. His guidance she obeyed as events unfolded and Delmar walked away from her. She realized a Christian must rely on Jesus' leading and not on one's own desires. He waits to show His path.

The rustle of a Sunday dress accompanied by a faint smell of rose water indicated that Augusta had entered the room. Not ready to talk, Cecily didn't acknowledge her.

Augusta, never one to let silent hints override her eagerness to find out the truth, didn't wait for Cecily to start speaking. "So, what happened?" Augusta's voice held an edge of uneasiness as she drew back the curtain to watch the departing suitor. "Delmar doesn't look too happy."

"I know." Cecily noticed that Delmar seemed to be observing his feet as he walked away.

"Uh-oh. It must not have been good. So he still didn't propose? What's he waiting for?" Augusta let out an exasperated breath.

Cecily looked over the top of Augusta's chignon to a small tintype of Aunt Agnes that had been a fixture on the wall as long as she could remember. Her deceased aunt's stare seemed to reprimand her. Cecily swallowed, determined to ignore the imagined reproof.

149

"He did propose. Yesterday." Her voice was barely above a whisper.

Augusta clapped her hand to her mouth. The sound brought Cecily to full attention. "Yesterday! Why didn't you say anything?" She moved her hands to her hips. "How could you keep such a big secret from me? I thought we always told each other everything!"

"I know, but. . ." Augusta's emphatic reaction left Cecily wishing she hadn't been so candid. "Well. . .I uh. . ."

"Cecily, you're not saying you. . ." Augusta's eyes were so wide that Cecily thought they would pop right out of their sockets. "You didn't turn him down, did you?"

Cecily wished she didn't have to admit to Augusta the truth. If breaking the news to her sister was this difficult, how could she possibly tell Mother?

"This is just what I was afraid of," Cecily said in her defense. "I knew you would try to convince me to marry him. And well, I knew I wasn't going to accept his proposal."

"What do you mean?" Augusta held her arms straight at her sides and clenched her fists in obvious frustration. "Cecily, how could you?"

"How could I? You act as though you're crazy about Delmar." Cecily tossed her head dismissively. "If you like him so much, then why don't you have Father invite him to court you? Delmar suggested as much when I told him I wouldn't be his wife."

"You're just saying that! You know I don't want him!" Augusta exclaimed. "I've always looked upon Delmar as my future brother-in-law. The notion of courting him is, well, too fantastical to contemplate." She looked into Cecily's eyes. "I'm not the one who's supposed to marry him. I'm not the one who's giving up a perfectly good match in exchange for an infatuation with a door-to-door salesman!"

Cecily clamped her mouth shut to keep from saying something to her sister that she might later lament.

"Not that there's anything wrong with selling pneumatic carpet renovators, mind you, but aside from bidding on your box, Mr. Kingsley hasn't made his intentions clear."

"He did escort me to the festivities," Cecily reminded her.

"Only to leave early." Augusta sniffed.

"On business."

The clacking heels of Mother's Sunday shoes sounding from the hall urged the sisters to calm themselves. By the time she crossed the doorway of the parlor, Cecily and Augusta had adopted poker faces. Upon crossing the threshold into the parlor, Mother narrowed her eyes and cocked her head in a scolding manner. "Girls! What is going on in here?"

"Nothing, Mother," they said in unison.

"It sounded as though you were arguing." She placed her hands on her hips, a gesture she shared with Augusta when exasperated. "What happened? I sent out the pie, but Hattie came back with it untouched. Why did Delmar leave without eating? That's not like him at all."

Father strode up behind Mother. "I was wondering the same thing. I've never known Delmar to pass up a dessert. Is he ill? Or is he just too much in love to eat anymore?" Father's teasing smile would have been welcome at any other time, but at the moment, his jesting only filled Cecily with guilt.

Cecily tried to look into the faces of her parents but found herself staring at Father's tie instead. Anything to keep from peering into their eyes. "I told him to leave," she muttered.

"My dear." Mother rushed to Cecily's side and put a comforting hand on her shoulder. "So he didn't speak up?"

Cecily hesitated. With all her might, she wanted to avoid telling her parents the truth, but she had no choice. The time had come.

*Father in heaven, please give me strength.*

"He did," she admitted.

Mother's mouth opened, and she took in a breath with such

force that Cecily thought she might fly out of the room. "How wonderful! After all this time. Well, we must immediately make arrangements! When is the date? This summer, perhaps?" She set her eyes on the adjacent wall in the direction of Mrs. MacGregor's house. "I must tell—"

"No!" Cecily said with enough emphasis to stop Mother's frantic train of thought. "It's not what you think. I turned him down."

Mother stopped cold. "Turned him down?" She rushed to the sofa and plopped onto a generous cushion. Father took a seat beside her.

"He proposed yesterday," Cecily admitted.

"Yesterday?" Mother and Father said in unison.

"Yes." Cecily faced her parents. "I'm sorry I didn't say anything before. I should have given Delmar his answer yesterday and saved everyone a lot of trouble, but I couldn't. He insisted I take some time to think about it. I did, and I prayed about it. I just don't feel led to marry Delmar."

Mother's eyes widened. "Even if it means you'll always be a. . .a. . ."

"Spinster," Cecily concluded. "Yes. I've decided I'd rather be a spinster than live out my life with a man who isn't the one for me."

"She's waiting for Mr. Kingsley," Augusta noted.

"I never said that," Cecily blurted. She pursed her lips and narrowed her eyes at Augusta, who in turn began to study the portrait of Grandmother Eaton that hung over the fireplace mantle.

Cecily shifted her gaze to her parents' faces. Mother's was clouded with distress, while Father's remained difficult to read. She wished they would say something. Anything. Why not go ahead and tell her that she was a terrible daughter, that their hurt and shame knew no bounds? Or they could say they would never be able to face their friends now that their daughter had turned away a man everyone else in the city thought a flawless suitor, a perfect match between the families and principles involved. Maybe they could even tell Cecily they would have to send her to the mountains in the southwest part of the state to live with her awful Aunt Fanny—perhaps to find a new suitor there. Cecily shuddered.

Her parents' reaction, or lack thereof, was much worse than anything they could have said.

Father broke the quiet. "Cecily, I know I speak for your mother as well as myself when I say how proud we are of you."

Cecily felt her mouth drop open. "You are?"

"Yes. It takes courage to take a chance on being a spinster for the rest of your life, to look beyond one's pride and turn away a man we all thought was right for you."

"Especially considering you may never have another chance," Mother added.

Father squeezed Mother around the shoulders with one arm. "Cecily, I love your mother very much, and I know she feels the same about me. Neither of us would wish anything less than a lifetime in a loving marriage for you."

Cecily watched Mother swallow. Her face softened as the impact of Father's words set in. After a moment, she nodded. "He's right, Cecily. I would rather see you not marry at all than see you unhappy and in a union that is less than what God intended when He instituted marriage in the Garden of Eden."

"Thank you." Cecily's voice was just above a whisper. Now that her parents had expressed their support of her decision, a sense of liberty washed over her.

"Well now." Father squeezed Mother once more. He let her go and plastered a smile on his face. "I don't know about the rest of you, but I don't plan to let two perfectly good slices of cherry pie go to waste. Anyone with me?" He looked at the three women in anticipation.

"Call Roger in. I'm sure he'll be happy to finish the pie with you," Mother advised. "I have some letters to write." As she disappeared, Cecily felt some of her earlier burden return. Her dismissal of Delmar had served her mother a defeat, one she wouldn't recover from too soon.

"Tell Aunt Fanny I said hello." Augusta's voice emanated too much sunshine.

"I have some things to do myself." Cecily took steps to follow her mother out of the room.

"Like, tell Mr. Kingsley that you're available?" Augusta whispered.

"No. And even if I had such plans, I wouldn't share them with you."

"Don't be mad. I don't blame you for liking Mr. Kingsley. Really I don't. And you said yourself he won't be a door-to-door salesman forever." Augusta patted her shoulder. "I'm sure he'll win Mother and Father over. One day. One day soon, I hope."

Cecily's heart felt lighter at the very thought.

⋙

"My, my," Father said as Cecily entered the kitchen for breakfast the following morning. "You girls will never believe what came in this morning's mail."

"I don't care what anyone says. I tell you, I'm innocent," Roger joked as he buttered a piece of toast.

"If only we could believe that," Augusta jested in return. She slid into her seat. "What is it, Father?"

He withdrew a piece of mail from the stack. Cecily was about to sit down but stood in place when she recognized the stilted and cramped handwriting on the envelope.

"It's a letter from Delmar," Father confirmed.

"A letter from Delmar?" Mother asked, breezing into the room. "Don't keep us in suspense, Dear. What does he say? Has he changed his mind? Is he going to give our Cecily another chance?" Her voice quickened its pace, but she managed to take her place at the end of the table.

Cecily tried not to flinch as she sat beside Mother. After

everything that had transpired the previous day, how could anyone think a match was possible? Leave it to Mother never to give up hope.

Father studied the letter as though trying to memorize its contents. "No." He shook his head. "Delmar has asked permission to court Augusta."

"What? Let me see that." Mother took the letter and read it for herself. Her face registered shock, then indignation. With a slow, sad gesture, she set the missive on the table and shook her head.

"Say," Roger interrupted, "I know this is an outrage, but does it mean we have to quit eating? I'm starved, and I promised the fellows I'd meet them at the gymnasium in fifteen minutes."

"I will not have you consuming your breakfast that quickly," Mother admonished. "Your friends can wait."

"Yes, Mother," he mumbled.

"Let's have our prayer," Father advised, which led his family to bow their heads for a word of grace.

Cecily barely listened to the short message of thanks sent up to God for His bountiful provision. She was too eager to return to the subject at hand. "I'm not surprised by Delmar. He as much as told me yesterday that he would ask to court Augusta." She passed a platter of steaming hot sausage and scrambled eggs flavored with cheddar cheese to her sister. "Didn't I tell you so?"

Augusta nodded. Cecily noted that her sister's eyes were so wide they seemed to consume her face.

"Not that I really believed him, mind you," Cecily confessed as she scooped a small portion of scrambled eggs onto her plate. "I thought perhaps he was speaking in the heat of the moment."

"I can't believe it," Augusta said. "Delmar? And me? The thought seems comical."

"You don't have to spare my feelings," Cecily interrupted. "If you want to see Delmar, it's fine with me."

Augusta shook her head. "I mean it. I want nothing to do with him. Ever."

"Good," Father said. "Imagine the nerve! To think that one sister is interchangeable with another." A sad expression overcame his features. "Cecily, apparently you are a superb judge of character."

Cecily nodded but not with a feeling of triumph.

Augusta set down a platter of bacon with a decisive thud. "If he comes to call, I shall instruct Hattie to tell him that I am not at home."

"You shall do no such thing," Father warned. "You know very well that the Ten Commandments forbid us to bear false witness."

Augusta looked down at the table. "I'm sorry, Father. If he comes to call, then I–I'll think of something."

Mother placed her hand on Cecily's. "I'm just glad he revealed his true colors before it was too late."

"Me too."

Mother took a sip of tea and then set down her cup with a deliberate motion. "Perhaps it's time I didn't try to influence your decision about what match to make. Obviously you are mature enough to discern for yourself."

Cecily realized how difficult such an admission was to make for a proud woman like her mother. "But not without the Lord's help," Cecily was more than willing to acknowledge.

"So true," Mother agreed.

"Yeah," Roger chimed between bites of bacon. "I never liked Delmar anyway. I think the carpet renovator salesman would be better. Isn't he sweet on you?"

The whole family chuckled. Though Cecily felt her cheeks burn hot, her relief transcended her embarrassment. Their laughter was a sure indication that at least they were no longer opposed to Averil.

*Maybe I haven't given my parents enough credit. So what if*

*Averil is merely a door-to-door salesman? I know he'll never make as much money as Delmar, and I'm sure he has no family trust fund to rely on. That's what really has my parents worried. I just know it. What they don't realize is, I can make do on any salary. Averil is kind and a gentleman. And he is equally yoked with me. And I love him. What more could any girl wish for?*

Cecily crumpled her napkin. At that moment, she couldn't remember a time when she had been more grateful that her family couldn't read her musings. What was she thinking? Why, she had let her mind stray far beyond any promises, or hint of a promise, that Averil had made.

# fourteen

Averil couldn't remember a time when he hadn't looked forward to delivering a Capital Duster Electric Pneumatic Carpet Renovator with a complete set of deluxe attachments. Under any other circumstances, he anticipated the smile of delight that always greeted him when he presented the shiny new machine in all its glory to a happy customer. Averil would make quite a show of the event. He would plug in the carpet renovator with aplomb, flip the "on" switch, then clean the customer's front room rug so it looked as clean and new as the carpet renovator itself.

An order that included deluxe attachments guaranteed a free cleaning of at least one sofa or chaise lounge as well, or even a room full of furniture if Averil was feeling especially industrious and generous. By the time he tipped his hat to wish the happy patron a good day, smiles covered every face in view.

But on this day, as he made his way down the street, he had no energy or desire to crack a smile nor to clean anything. He looked upon his next stop with dread. As he led the carriage to the Eatons', he knew he had to do his best to treat them with the respect and enthusiasm with which he would greet any other customer.

*I hope Cecily isn't there. Or if she is, I pray I can avoid her. Perhaps she's at a church meeting or seeing friends.* He even would have welcomed the prospect of her taking another music lesson with Professor Tobias. Anything to avoid seeing her, now that she was in all probability engaged to someone else.

Or would he?

No. He would put on a happy face, deliver the carpet renovator, and if Miss Cecily were home, he would wish her well. That is what he would do.

"Yes. Yes I will." His feelings were so adamant that he expressed them aloud. "You won't tell anybody how crazy I am, will you, General?" he asked his horse. "I don't know about you, Major," he said to the new horse he had purchased now that he needed to get around by carriage. "You know, around here, we don't betray one another's confidences."

He sighed. He must be lonely to talk to his horses. And in public, at that.

Eyeing a portly man dressed in a morning suit, he recognized the man as Mr. Wilson, a prospect who had turned him down cold just two days before. Nevertheless, Averil smiled and tipped his hat. He always made a point to be friendly to everyone, even those who turned down a chance to buy a renovator. "My good old-fashioned pump model has served me well for twenty years," Mr. Wilson had said. "And I imagine it'll serve me another twenty just as fine."

Averil had left Mr. Wilson a business card all the same. As soon as he was out of earshot, Averil told his horses, "He'll be back. Just you wait and see."

Major whinnied.

"Good boy. I can see we will get along splendidly."

Averil's mood dampened as he pulled up to the Eatons' drive. If only he felt as cheerful as he tried to portray by his expression. As much as he wished he could ask Mr. Eaton for the privilege of courting Cecily, he couldn't. He would not interfere in her commitments.

Averil tied the horses to the hitching post, opened the wagon door, and lugged the machine out the back. For the tenth time, he resolved not to promise that the renovator was light as a feather. Perhaps it was light in comparison to older models, but. . .

"Do you need some help with that, Mr. Kingsley?"

❧

"Oh!" Augusta's voice rang through the house. "Look who's talking to Mr. Kingsley!"

"He's here?" Cecily jumped from her perch on the piano bench. She had been practicing "Oh for a Thousand Tongues to Sing" to play in church the following week while the organist, Mrs. Watson, planned to be away visiting her daughter in Alexandria.

Without a moment's pause, she ran to the window. Augusta was sitting backward on the couch, propped up on both knees, a posture she had used to spy out the window ever since she was a child. Feeling rather childish herself for spying on activities taking place on her own front lawn, Cecily joined her sister in an identical pose.

"Of course he's here. He was supposed to deliver the carpet renovator today, remember?"

Cecily swallowed. She remembered.

"I wonder what Professor Tobias is saying to him?"

Cecily studied the slight figure beside Averil. Though she had at first thought him short, Averil looked like Goliath in comparison to the diminutive music teacher. And what a handsome Goliath indeed! As always, Averil cut a fine figure in his business suit and derby hat. Standing straight, he looked every bit the hero. If she had been made of sugar instead of flesh and blood, Cecily knew her heart would have melted at the sight of him.

"Isn't he so very dashing and handsome?" Augusta said.

"Yes, Averil is." Cecily clasped her hands to her chest.

"You mean, Mr. Kingsley?" Augusta shrugged. "I suppose he is. But I meant Professor Tobias."

Cecily shook her head. "How can you think that, after he's been so inconsiderate of your feelings?"

Augusta sighed. "I don't know. How can you argue with love?"

"How can you, indeed?" Cecily mused. She loved Averil

Kingsley. There was no argument about that. "Speaking of arguments, it looks like they are in a heated debate of some sort." Cecily felt her heart's beating increase.

"Really?" Augusta leaned so closely to the screen that her nose touched it. "You're right. Neither of them looks very happy. I wish I could hear what they're saying." She moved her head so her ear pressed against the screen. "Now I can hear much better!"

Cecily shushed her sister. "If we don't quiet down, they'll be the ones listening to us. And that would be embarrassing."

"Not any more embarrassing than if they break out into a fight right here and now," Augusta pointed out. "And from what I can tell, your Mr. Kingsley looks as though he'd like to wring Professor Tobias's neck." Slack jawed, she looked at Cecily. "Do you suppose we should go out there and stop them?"

"I don't think so." Cecily placed a restraining hand on Augusta's arm. "Whatever their argument is, they'd better settle it for themselves."

*

Averil knew the voice was familiar, but he couldn't place its owner. Who was it? He turned and discovered Professor Tobias. The anemic-looking young man appeared as though he would have difficulty lifting a piece of lint, much less a hearty machine like the carpet renovator.

"It's you," Averil said.

Professor Tobias tipped his hat. "You seem surprised."

Averil supposed he was, but etiquette demanded that he compose himself enough to tip his hat in return. "Good morning, Professor Tobias. And thank you, but no. I'm coping quite well." To prove his point, he removed the renovator from the buggy in one smooth motion.

"If you say so."

Averil wondered how he had managed to run into Professor Tobias at the Eatons'. He set the machine beside the buggy and beamed at the teacher. "So, this is a mighty fine afternoon to be out and about. Have the Misses Eaton consented to resume music lessons with you?"

"No, that is not the reason for my visit." His jaw tightened. "I am here to call upon Miss Cecily Eaton."

"Miss Cecily? Did I hear you correctly?" Averil stifled a chuckle.

"Yes, you did."

Averil didn't know how to respond. Cecily's lack of interest in the music teacher had been obvious at the picnic. Hadn't the man seen that?

"I hope your delivery of the carpet machine is your sole purpose for stopping by here today," Professor Tobias observed.

"Yes, it is." He was unable to keep regret from seeping through his voice. Averil looked at the new machine as though he had never seen such a marvel.

"Good," Professor Tobias answered. "I'll have you know that your presence here is not welcome for any other purpose."

His remark caused Averil to snap his head in Professor Tobias's direction. "So Mr. Eaton has granted you explicit permission to court his daughter?"

He hesitated. "No. I'm just stopping by on my way from a music lesson a few blocks away." The teacher nodded his head toward a leather satchel he carried, which Averil surmised contained sheets of music. "Today's visit is informal, just a pleasant call to pass the time of day. But my intentions are honorable. I do plan to ask Mr. Eaton's permission to court Miss Eaton soon. And I am confident he will heartily agree." Professor Tobias puffed out his chest.

"Are you really so sure of that?"

"Of course." Nevertheless, Professor Tobias's voice quivered ever so slightly.

"But how can you expect to court Miss Cecily when she is being courted by Mr. Delmar Williams?"

"I have heard no such thing," Professor Tobias responded. "Of course, everyone knows that neither Mr. and Mrs. Eaton nor Mr. and Mrs. Williams would be opposed to such a match. They have even encouraged it, in fact. But nothing is formal. Both sisters have assured me so many times."

"Indeed? That isn't the impression I received from Miss Augusta."

"Remember, Mr. Kingsley, you are but a stranger to us yet," Professor Tobias said with no small amount of pride coloring his voice. "I am much more privy to the details of their lives than are you." He leaned toward Averil and lowered his voice as though sharing a confidence. "You see, I have spent quite a bit of time with both sisters."

Averil bristled. "In your capacity as a music teacher."

Professor Tobias leaned back. "Obviously, you have no idea how friendly teachers and their students might become, given the proper circumstances."

Averil opened his mouth to object, but Professor Tobias ignored him.

"In any event, if Miss Cecily were a betrothed woman in love, wouldn't she have let every man in the world know about it?"

Averil didn't answer right away. Professor Tobias's logic was too sensible to debate.

"So, it stands to reason, my good man, that if you believe you are here to perform any task other than the delivery of their purchase, think again." Professor Tobias gave the machine a dismissive look and then swayed from side to side in a superior manner. "Clearly I am the man in the elder Miss Eaton's future."

"I haven't heard her say any such thing."

"Not yet. But she will," he said, lifting a forefinger to the blue sky. "I plan to marry her one day. One day in the not-too-distant future."

"Marry her?" Averil knew that the purpose of a formal court-ship was to marry, but the full impact of Professor Tobias's intentions didn't register with him until the words fell from his lips.

"Yes." A triumphant grin lingered over the music teacher's face. "But. . .but. . ."

"But what?" Professor Tobias seemed to be enjoying himself far too much.

Averil felt the heat of anger rise in his chest. "You can't marry her. I love her!" he burst out.

The teacher's mouth dropped open to such an extent that Averil wondered if it would ever close again. "You. . .you what?"

Averil hadn't realized the depth of his emotions until that moment. And he had to go and shout it out to the music teacher, of all people. What was he thinking? No, that was just the problem. He hadn't been thinking. He hadn't been thinking at all. He decided not to repeat himself.

"That is the most preposterous notion I've ever heard," Professor Tobias said. "So preposterous, you can't even bear to say it again."

Challenged, Averil was determined to prove the teacher wrong, even at the cost of his own pride. He forced himself to repeat his sentiment. "Yes, I can. I love Cecily Eaton, and there's not a thing you can do about that." His voice sounded louder than he intended.

"Yell all you like," the teacher conceded, his voice brittle. "But that doesn't mean you can court her." Professor Tobias cocked his head toward the Eaton house. "Don't you realize that even if she agreed to see you, her family would never accept a traveling salesman as a suitor for their eldest daughter?"

Remembering the chilly reception he had received from Mrs. Eaton, Averil wondered if Professor Tobias's words didn't contain a smidgen of truth. Still, he had to protest. "I take exception to your comment, Sir!"

Professor Tobias took one step back before he spoke again. "How dare you take exception! If you could see plainly, you would know you have nothing to offer a woman of Cecily's culture and refinement."

"I have plenty of culture and refinement. My family holds season tickets to the theater, and I attended the finest schools in New York."

"New York." The teacher sniffed. "Yes. Of course, you can be pardoned for wanting to climb the social ladder, but I'm afraid you've chosen the wrong people this time. You'll have to take your ladder elsewhere."

Averil balled his hands into tight fists but controlled the urge to raise them as a challenge to fight. Never in his life had he been accused of being a social climber. He wasn't sure how to respond to such a ridiculous notion. "The fact of the matter is, Professor Tobias," he said, being careful to keep his tone even, "my family is quite prominent in the state of New York."

"I am too much a gentleman to dispute your word, but any prestige you might enjoy there has no bearing whatsoever here."

"Perhaps that is so. Naturally, the Kingsley name wouldn't hold as much sway among people who aren't acquainted with us and our fine history. But now you listen to me. I'll have you know that my own mother is a member of the Dames of the Magna Carta." Averil didn't mind that a sense of satisfaction permeated his voice.

Professor Tobias's eyebrows lifted as high as Averil supposed was possible. "You mean to say you can trace your roots back to thirteenth-century England?"

"Yes, we can," Averil said. "And I'm sure that fact speaks well of my family regardless of where we live."

"My membership in the Sons of Confederate Veterans speaks well enough of me." The professor twisted his mouth into a sardonic line. "I don't quite imagine any of your relatives fought on the side of the Confederacy in the War Between the States?"

"I don't need the Confederacy! I am heir to the Capital Duster Company!" Averil raised his index finger. "And I assure you, Professor Tobias, that fact gains me entrance into some of the finest homes in the country!"

"What did you say?"

"I said—" Averil stopped himself. Had he just told Professor Tobias that he was heir to his father's company? He groaned inwardly. "Never mind what I said."

"Anything said that is not worth repeating is nothing less than a lie." The music teacher clenched his fists. "Why, if I weren't a gentleman, you'd soon find yourself lying flat on the street right here and now!"

"Is that so?" Averil held back a laugh. He suspected Professor Tobias's spindly physique was the real reason he exercised such control. Had Averil chosen to take a swipe at him, Professor Tobias was the one who'd be lying on the street.

"You're right about that!" the teacher assured him, although his voice didn't hold as much bravado as before. "I may not look so tough, but you don't want to try me."

Averil looked at the Eatons' house. He could imagine how the tongues of local gossips would wag upon learning that two grown men engaged in fisticuffs on the Eatons' front lawn. What would he look like, delivering a new carpet renovator in a torn and dirtied suit? If he were to come to blows with Cecily's former music instructor, he knew Cecily and her family would be convinced that Averil was no gentleman, no matter how large or significant his inheritance might be.

"You're right," he conceded to Professor Tobias. "I don't want to try you. There is no need for a second Civil War. I suggest that we treat each other as the gentlemen we are. Why don't you say we call a truce?" He extended his hand in reconciliation.

Professor Tobias unclenched his hands and set them at his sides. "Well, if you say so. I don't blame you for not wanting to fight me." With a hesitant motion, he extended his hand in return.

"That's the spirit!" Averil said, all the while knowing his pride was controlling his tongue. "How would it look for us to fight out here in broad daylight?" He chuckled.

Professor Tobias swept his glance over the neighborhood. "Not too gentlemanly, I suppose."

"Let me make another proposal. If Miss Cecily chooses you, I'll gladly step aside."

"She already has."

"Really?" Averil's voice held more bravado than he felt. Fact of the matter was, he couldn't guarantee Cecily would have anything to do with him. He hadn't seen her since the picnic. What was she feeling? What was she thinking?

"Why don't we go inside right here and now and find out?" Professor Tobias suggested. "We can ask her to choose between us."

"Averil!"

"Cecily!" He whipped his head toward the verandah. Cecily was practically running across the lawn toward them.

At that moment, any doubt he had about Cecily evaporated. How could he have even entertained the slightest notion that she could hide anything from him? Judging from her enthusiasm, his worst nightmare had not materialized. She hadn't become engaged to Delmar Williams, after all. He almost collapsed with relief.

As she approached, Professor Tobias tipped his hat. "Please, Miss Eaton, I can explain everything. This man here, this vile creature—"

Cecily didn't so much as glance in the teacher's direction. "This vile creature is the man I love!"

"Love?" A combination of embarrassment, fear, and exaltation pulsed through the core of Averil's being.

"Yes, love." Her brown eyes sparkled, their golden flecks ever more apparent in the light of day.

Averil gulped. "You heard me?"

"We heard everything," Augusta's voice interrupted. Having run across the lawn after her sister, she was winded but coherent. "We even heard that you're not really a door-to-door salesman after all. At least, not forever." She put her hands on her hips. "Mr. Kingsley, why didn't you tell us you are heir to the company?"

"He is?" Cecily's eyes grew wide, and her mouth dropped open.

Augusta quickly jumped in. "You didn't hear that? Mr. Kingsley is heir to his father's company. He'll be president of Capital Dusters one day."

"Oh," Cecily uttered. "I guess I wasn't paying attention. I stopped listening after you said you love me. That is what you said, isn't it?"

"Yes." He was more than happy to repeat those sentiments. Averil rushed to her and embraced her with a passion he didn't realize he possessed. "I love you, Cecily. I've loved you since the day I first saw you. And I always will."

"And I love you, Averil." Her eyes were alight with emotion as she returned his embrace.

"I nearly had to tie her down to keep her from running out here as soon as you told the professor," Augusta said. "But I'm glad I made her wait. Mr. Kingsley's future is secure. Now there's nothing Mother or Father can object to!"

"Nothing," Professor Tobias whispered. "Nothing at all." His face slackened with obvious disappointment.

Augusta tugged at his sleeve. "You know something, Professor Tobias? I'm having the most trouble with one of Beethoven's sonatas. Won't you come in the music room with me for just a moment? Perhaps you could help me over the rough spots."

Professor Tobias looked too stunned to know a high C from a B flat.

Augusta batted her eyelashes. "Won't you? Pretty please?"

The music teacher stared blankly at Cecily and Averil for a

moment. "I, well, I suppose I could take a moment. . . ."

"Good!" Augusta said.

Still holding Cecily, Averil watched as Augusta tugged with so much force that he thought she was sure to pull the sleeve right off the professor's suit coat.

Cecily squeezed Averil's waist, focusing his attention back where it belonged—upon her. She looked into his eyes. "Averil, don't you see? I don't care whether you're a door-to-door salesman or the most important man in the world. All I care about is you."

"Then I can ask your father for permission to court you?"

"Yes!" Cecily exclaimed. "A thousand times, yes!"

The anticipation in her face made her appear lovelier than ever. Averil nodded. A sudden feeling of overwhelming gratitude and humility enveloped him. "I don't care what my inheritance is. As much as I love you, I'm not worthy of you, Cecily."

"Don't say that. I think you are."

"But—"

Averil watched as Cecily's face moved toward his own. When her lips touched his, he couldn't remember a sweeter moment. Everything else dissolved, everything except Cecily, as he wrapped his arms around her waist more tightly and returned her ardor.

All too soon, the moment was interrupted. "Cecily!"

The sound of her mother's voice caused them to break their hold on one another.

"Cecily! What are you thinking, putting on such a scandalous display here in broad daylight for all the world to see? Will you not honor convention?"

"Convention?" she scoffed. "I've been conventional long enough. Living by the expectations of others almost led me to marry the wrong man. For once I'm doing exactly what I want. Something I've wanted to do for a very long time."

She turned her face back to Averil. The approval in his eyes was all she needed. As he moved his face toward hers for another kiss, Cecily knew with no uncertainty that the new course she had set for her life was one that would be right forever.

# A Letter To Our Readers

Dear Reader:

In order that we might better contribute to your reading enjoyment, we would appreciate your taking a few minutes to respond to the following questions. We welcome your comments and read each form and letter we receive. When completed, please return to the following:

Fiction Editor
Heartsong Presents
PO Box 719
Uhrichsville, Ohio 44683

1. Did you enjoy reading *Loveswept* by Tamela Hancock Murray?
   ❏ Very much! I would like to see more books by this author!
   ❏ Moderately. I would have enjoyed it more if

   _____

   _____

   _____

2. Are you a member of **Heartsong Presents**?  ❏ Yes  ❏ No
   If no, where did you purchase this book? _____

   _____

3. How would you rate, on a scale from 1 (poor) to 5 (superior), the cover design? _____

4. On a scale from 1 (poor) to 10 (superior), please rate the following elements.

   ____ Heroine              ____ Plot
   ____ Hero                 ____ Inspirational theme
   ____ Setting              ____ Secondary characters

5. These characters were special because?_____
_____
_____

6. How has this book inspired your life?_____
_____
_____

7. What settings would you like to see covered in future
**Heartsong Presents** books? _____
_____
_____

8. What are some inspirational themes you would like to see
treated in future books? _____
_____
_____

9. Would you be interested in reading other   **Heartsong
Presents** titles?  ❏ Yes   ❏ No

10.  Please check your age range:
    ❏ Under 18          ❏ 18-24
    ❏ 25-34             ❏ 35-45
    ❏ 46-55             ❏ Over 55

Name_____

Occupation _____

Address _____

City_____ State_____ Zip_____

# AUSTRALIAN OUTBACK

## 4 stories in 1

*P*opulated by those unwanted by "proper" society—and by those willing to pursue love around the world—Australia began to flourish in the early 1800s. Now, lifelong Australian Mary Hawkins brings these brave Aussie characters to life.

Can four couples discover a deepening faith and a lasting love while tackling the challenges of life in the Australian outback? Will they find that no land is too wild for God?

Historical, paperback, 480 pages, 5 ³/₁₆"x 8"

# Presents